THESE
RESTLESS
HEADS

THESE
RESTLESS HEADS

A Trilogy of Romantics

BY BRANCH CABELL

"Yet must there hover in these restless heads
One thought, one grace, one wonder, at the least,
Which into words no virtue can digest."

DECORATIVE ILLUSTRATIONS
SAMUEL BERNARD SCHAEFFER

ROBERT M. McBRIDE & COMPANY
NEW YORK : MCMXXXII

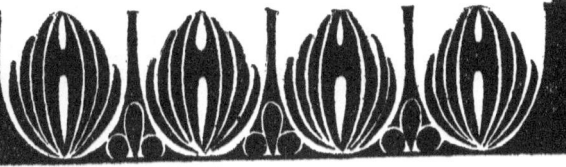

THESE RESTLESS HEADS

PRINTED IN THE UNITED STATES OF AMERICA

For

JOHN MACY

Journeys end in lovers meeting;
Only June may follow May;
Hearts like muffled drums are beating;
Not a dog but has his day.

Absence makes the heart grow fonder;
Learn to look before you leap;
Blondes are better yet when blonder;
Early sow and early reap.

Rules like these, with others not of
Themes less varied, I pursue
Mindful of what more I wot of
Axioms thus trite yet true
Controverted by a lot of
Younger folk than I or you.

CONTENTS

Contents

INTRODUCTION

KO-KO. *In the first place, self-decapitation is an extremely difficult, not to say dangerous, thing to attempt; and, in the second, it's suicide, and suicide is a capital offence. Besides, I don't see how a man can cut off his own head.*

POOH-BAH. *A man might try.*

I T may be observed (by the over careful about trifles) that with the present volume the author's name has suffered truncation. The main cause of this change is my desire, for the reasons explained in *Townsend of Lichfield*, to distinguish as sharply as may be between those volumes which make up the Biography of the life of Manuel and such other publishings as under the dictates of chance I may or may not emit; and thus in some sort to emphasize still again the circumstance that the Biography is one single, one continuous, and one indivisible book.

This fact as yet requires emphasizing, I discover, in a tender-minded world, which cannot well reflect upon the inhumanity of books in eighteen volumes without some natural and extreme discomfort,—and which so (rather than face the disturbing thought) would by much prefer to exonerate their contriver, even in the bared teeth of his unrepentant confession, by declining to consider his confession. This is a charitableness which one may appreciate without accepting: and such is my chosen course. It is the course here signalized by allotting to the Biography in plain terms its own exclusive author; and by limiting the output of this now delimited writer to the Biography alone.

For yet another affair I am minded to render (through the time-hallowed gentleman's quietus of beheadment) the literary career of my predecessor unique, in that his Collected Works must now stand, and so perish by-and-by, in the exact form he designed and completed,—without any guesswork as to his final plans and with no blunders save his own, with no inclusions untivitated by him, with no loose ends anywhere, with no incongruous editing by other hands, and (above all) with no lackwit replevinings from his waste-paper basket conducted by his heirs and creditors. If any other writer has escaped all these provokers of discursive parody after death (except of course through a worthlessness so patent as to defy republication) I do not know of him.

My predecessor evades each of these ills. And I cry farewell to the author of the Biography with some unavoidable sorrow that the perfection attained by his career was not shared by his book.

As concerns the present book I needs speak even more briefly. The Prologue and the Epilogue when regarded as units seem to require no explaining and to deride connection. Elsewhere in this book, as should be remarked by the student of local color, I have but followed the supremely otiose plan of writing about whatsoever objects might happen to be immediately in front of me when I took my accustomed seat during, severally, a spring morning, a summer day, an autumn afternoon, and a winter's night.

By the straitly rational the result must be adjudged a batch of disconnected papers. Yet I elect to believe some less logical persons, here and there, may perceive that this book is in fact, as its title page has indicated, a cohering trilogy which concerns itself, after its own fashion, with one single main theme and with one protagonist.

Cayford Cottage
July 1931

PROLOGUE OF
DUKE PROSPERO
AT MILAN

Why, that's my dainty Ariel! I shall miss thee;
But yet thou shalt have freedom: so, so, so.

1

Reflections on an Island

HE story of Duke Pros-
pero of Milan remains
generally known, even
to those of us whom
time has mercifully re-
leased from the class-
room. Yet we encounter him only in the flush of
triumph, lifted to a complacent mood of forgive-
ness: and the six hours' action of his revealed
history is regarded through specially colored
spectacles, in that its participants move, as it
were, about a landscape momentarily trans-
figured by the dawn of a new day: wherein
all is invested with strange glows and quiet
splendors and with the dawn's many happy acci-
dents of oblique lighting; wherein all that one
finds is pleasantly exceptional; and wherein all

3

very swiftly becomes changed under the sun's full touch.

Upon his Island Prospero had spent the fifteen years of his prime. No magic could restore to him that completion of manhood which had been wasted. He had looked back perforce, during the gray length of his exile, upon over-much of double-dealing and falseness, and upon the yet uglier fact that among his fellows he had won no affection beyond the cool charity of old Gonzalo. This fact begot poor thoughts of Prospero's talent for human living. He had been the supreme lord of wealthy and fertile Milan. He had lost the strong castles, the gay villas and treasure chambers and pleasant orchards of the courtly City of the Viper, through his drugged inattention to the plain needs of his dignity and through that dubiousness and that light but steadfast disliking with which practical-minded persons regard the recluse. The greed and treachery of knaves no doubt had speeded him toward this island; but his own incompetence had been the pilot.

He paid now for that incompetence in an extreme loneliness. His daughter, Miranda, as he reflected forlornly, was but another hen-headed piece of virtue: the girl lacked intelligence, and in all other ways she developed day by day into a painstaking likeness of her mother. Caliban too was unintellectual. Prospero felt—shrinkingly, with quiet desperation—that he lived among second-rate people. Yonder the large human world went on (unseen by the recluse, and uncomprehended by the recluse) in a proud whirl of splendor and noise and action: he was cooped here, between sand and palm-tree, with a dull-witted fond wench and a freckled savage, while life ebbed out of him.

Nor was Ariel any real comfort. Ariel served you nimbly: but at all times you found contempt in the eyes of this airy spirit, the contempt of an immortal bondman for the transient master, chance-given, who so very soon would not be living. Ariel would serve other human masters then, just as nimbly: meanwhile it was plain

5

that Ariel also regarded you with a dubiousness
and a light but steadfast disliking.

Equally little comfort was to be got of those
arts practised by the unfortunate and accomplished exile now that he had mastered the secret of the Sylphs. To attend upon these irrational mysteries and to deliver them exultingly
into form and color was an acceptable enough
diversion in his insular quiet: and this pagean-
try of bright nonsense appeared to him, at least
now and then, very well contrived. It was amusing, too, at times, to evoke the quaint music of
the Undines, or through the Elves' aid to bring
about a soothing eclipse of the sun or a brisk,
brilliantly designed thunderstorm; and with
white necromancy to summon up the simulacra
of dead persons was a form of nonsense which
permitted even more of dexterity and variousness. Yet as a creative artist Prospero, howsoever providentially blessed with the advantages
of contemporary criticism, from out of Caliban's
wide mouth, remained always that incomplete
creature, an artist who is without any audience.

2

The Triumph of Justice

FROM this long loneliness Duke Prospero was swept, as the world knows, by a tempest. With all evils righted, all wrongs forgiven, and Ariel set free from his servitude, Duke Prospero became again lord of Milan, ruling over the broad Lombard plain. He lacked for nothing in comfort, in wealth, nor in men's deference. He heard everywhere the world's benison, for they of King Alonso's court who had been shipwrecked upon the Island had cause to respect Duke Prospero: the fact that his dark art had been formally put aside was no guaranty that the sage might not, under some vexing provocation, resume its practice. They had over clearly seen what that art might achieve toward its beholders' discomfort. Those stay-at-homes who heard the tale of the wronged Duke's triumph

7

were well satisfied: their sense of justice was pleased, and righteousness had prevailed again very gloriously, without inconveniencing their private affairs.

Prospero lived as a great prince of Italy, with no liege lord save his own will and with no need to bother about that slight peculiarity which had developed in mirrors. He lacked time to bother about such trifles now that the Duke had turned, with something of the convert's extreme zeal, to all common-sense dealings. Duke Prospero was intent to make firm his part in the solidarity of human doings, after his over-long loneliness. His subjects found him a model of executive ability, with sound views as to agriculture and finance and the problems of sewerage: in every way he conformed to all which could be expected of a serious-minded duke. The laws of Milan were enforced with thoroughness and mercy, and a series of highly popular wars was inaugurated. With red porphyry and almond blossom marble and rose-colored tilings and much glowing terra-cotta, the

prospering city of Milan was rebuilded throughout by its never-idle overlord. The orations of
the Duke whensoever he addressed a loyal popu-
lace in the Duomo were of a decorous dullness:
he gave liberally to the Church, patronizing im-
partially the most holy relic of the Sacred Nail
and the sublime Saints Ambrose and Lawrence
and Vincent; besides adding a silver and rock
crystal shrine to the Cathedral, he maintained
four mistresses upon such a scale of extrava-
gance as yet further fostered the fine arts and all
manufactures. In brief, there was never a Duke
of Milan who fulfilled the duties of his office
more efficiently, nor to more wide-spread applause: and the realm thrived in a bustling era
of militant success and commercial prosperity.

The artist was well pleased with his work. It
seemed to him that, no matter what any delusive
mirrors might be hinting, this decisive, all-over-
bearing but yet kindly man of affairs was really
a superb creation. Prospero would often medi-
tate after supper, in the soothing quiet of his
library, upon the sturdy common-sense deeds he

9

had performed during the day. He profoundly admired this Duke of Milan whom the sun's full touch revealed to be in all matters successful and practical. This Duke was Prospero's masterpiece in a new field. Prospero played now with quite solid human beings just as on the Island he had played with small Elves and with thin illusions, Duke Prospero would consider when he cast a short sideglance toward that irrational mirror; and the incurable artist had principalities and nations for his audience.

3

Annotations of Unreason

THE one trouble continued to be the deceiving-
ness of mirrors. He noticed that in mirrors he
found the sage and calm figure of an all-victori-
ous prince, but that this admirable figure regarded him with the bright, the slightly
malicious, and the contemptuous eyes of Ariel.
Duke Prospero could not see himself quite as
did his courtiers: and all mirrors began to trouble him more and yet more. These mirrors did
not enable him to observe himself with ease, but
instead seemed to betray him to the scrutiny
of another person, who was incuriously deriding
the great Duke of Milan.

He could not remain away from a mirror for
any long while. When his statecraft or his war-
faring was at rest for that season, when for the
instant there was no altruism to be performed

nobly, and in the pauses of his religious and amatory beneficence, Duke Prospero would return to his library and to his tall mirror. The figure which he regarded became more wasted and much older looking, as the months of loud triumphs and of ever-present applause went by, but he found no changing in the derisive cool eyes which regarded him.

Duke Prospero duly breathed toward the four cardinal points of the compass. He repeated the Prayer of the Sylphs. He wrote then upon the air, with the quill of an eagle's feather, the spell which controls airy spirits; but in the mirror he still faced the amused bright eyes of Ariel, whom he had released from all controls.

"Alas," said Duke Prospero, "I am now beleaguered by an airy spirit that does not regard properly the more solid affairs of human kind, nor the gold chain of my office hung about my neck. He whispers to me such thin nonsense as cannot ever beguile a well-thought-of nobleman with the gold chain of his office shining about his neck. There have been, this spirit assures me,

12

yet other Dukes of Milan who have strutted in such chains since the Visconti first got the better of the Torriani. My honors are torn goods re-patched: my laurels also have been worn a long while before I wore them, by many skulls, when each one of these other dukes was in his bypast day as important as I now seem in this day which is passing. Each had his wars and his desires and his mistresses and his statecraft: and whether he fared well or ill with them does not matter to the jumbled bones that are in his gilded coffin, and it does not matter to any man who goes alive in the sunlight. . . . But that is only a truism; and the well-thought-of do not think of such truisms as being true."

Then Duke Prospero said: "Each one of these well-thought-of dukes has postured and has spoken gravely and has listened to long applause in the while that he bustled about untiringly, like a gleaming fly that is exceedingly busy in his patch of sunlight until evening comes. It is now as though these dukes had never been. I can recall but a few of their names. I do not pause to

13

distinguish between that one of my forerunners
under the sun's full touch who got the better of
the Emperor Wencelaus and that one of my forerunners who perished miserably at Como in a
wooden cage, because nowadays there is not any
difference between them. Of this bustling in old
sunlights there remains only a little dust and a
name or a date which schoolmasters repeat, very
infrequently, without any interest. It is a large
folly, says my airy spirit, to be a well-thought-of
duke in Milan and to be wasting life upon the
solid affairs of human kind. . . . But that is
cheap pessimism; and the well-thought-of have
not any reason to think well of pessimism."

And Duke Prospero said also: "In my Island
many unborn dreams await to be delivered into
form and color, but here the doings of the applauded perish. They that prosper in my Milan
have not any dreams: they sleep in contentment
far too soundly for any dreams. Their snoring
becomes oracular. An airy spirit therefore de-
rides them without any mercy. Come away from
these wise doings, says my airy spirit, and let us

not strive any longer to guide the unicorn in double harness with the dray horse. Let us seek after a more delicate folly among the irrational Isles of Wonder. The true desire of your clouded heart is to follow after unborn dreams hopelessly: and no one of us who has learned the secret of the Sylphs may find any content in contentment. Come away, Duke Prospero, oh, come away; put aside the vainglories of common-sense for my harsh liveries; and let us hunt again after that which no man may attain to, so that you may meet oblivion after much wasted laboring. . . . But that is balderdash; and a world-famous duke has not any reason to think about oblivion."

Thereafter Duke Prospero laughed, and he said stoutly: "Such is the thin nonsense which my airy spirit whispers. With such nonsense would an upstart servant entrap me to become the drudge of this runagate spirit until my life's end. It is a nonsense which cannot ever beguile a well-thought-of nobleman with the gold chain of his office shining about his neck."

4

Leaves One at Sea

THESE matters are known. And it is known also
that when Duke Prospero knelt before the tall
mirror and prayed wildly, it seemed to him that
he must be weeping, for he could feel a trickling
warmth on his cheeks, and he could taste too the
salt of his tears: but the gray writhing madman
in the mirror had dry and lightly amused young
eyes.

Formerly, as Duke Prospero well remembered, these cool eyes had regarded him with
dubiousness and with a light but steadfast disliking: now they regarded him with amusement,
ruthlessly. Duke Prospero could over plainly
foresee that never-ending and cruel servitude
which awaited him upon his Island if once he
returned to it as the thrall of Ariel.

He rejoiced that there was no least need to

16

return. He heartened himself with red wine and with white wine, so that he might deride more merrily the foolishness of his discharged lackey. In the mirror swayed a disheveled gray sot: he waved a flagon frenziedly, as the sound token of his complete contentment, and he reviled and jeered at Ariel in a frightened screeching voice which Duke Prospero heard with offended distaste; but all the while this figure regarded Duke Prospero with sane and implacable eyes which remained lightly amused.

These matters, I repeat, are known. Yet the upshot of these matters is not known quite so certainly. The conservative have reported that upon a fine March morning Duke Prospero entered into eternal rest, under the proper medical attention, and that a funeral from his late residence at the Sforza Castle then wound up his earthly affairs without any further nonsense or any unbecoming scandal. Romanticists, however, have talked of a small boat which went seaward that spring, through the dawn of yet another new day, in the approved old style of outlandish adventuring. Above it, they declared, hovered a pair of favorable winds with cheeks puffed to the bursting point: small sea serpents curveted about the prow, which displayed as its figure-head a rearing stallion colored like silver: at each side of the boat three mermaids diversified the mild waves, in attitudes which dealt nobly with six praiseworthy bosoms. This boat contained only an aging man, whose face was not clearly seen, said these romanticists; but they believed he was Duke Prospero, the incurable artist, bent upon a return to the beauty and the nonsense of his Island.

*ABOUT THE POSTMAN
IN SPRING*

I am grown older by a great many years since my first publications: but I very much doubt whether I am grown an inch the wiser. I now, and I anon, are two several persons; but whether better, I cannot determine. It were a fine thing to be old, if we only travelled towards improvement; but 'tis a drunken, stumbling, reeling, infirm motion: like that of reeds, which the air casually waves to and fro at pleasure.

The Sublime Passing

 IS epiphany does by so much precede his advent that he becomes visible each morning a full half-hour before he arrives. While I sit yet at breakfast he is notable upon the other side of the street. He advances not as go unominous mortals, on the pavement, but on the low brick coping which borders the terraced yards; this spares him from ascending and descending the walkway steps at each house for which he has traffic: and through the fumes of my oatmeal I can observe our postman thus proceeding in the May sunlight, beneath the very pale green leaves of young oak-trees, for a considerable distance down Monument Avenue after much the fashion of an unhurried cat upon a fence top.

He returns to the asphalt pavement; and I
notice that in his official progress he leans well
to the left so as to offset the weight of the mail
pouch at his right side. This so affects his gait
that at first glance you might imagine his right
leg to be longer than its fellow and to be slightly
bowed. His aspect (as befits heaven's emissary)
is tinged with radiance. From afar may be observed the gleam of his eight brass buttons and
the intermittent shining of his cap's patent
leather visor and of the oval plate upon the front
of his cap: his steel-rimmed spectacles also re-
ject the morning sunlight sparklingly.

It is now apparent that since his birth he has
been of that blameless Ethiopian race with
whom the Hellenic gods most loved to inter-
change visits and to make merriment sitting at
the feast. Among our homes of merely Nordic
culture he treads with the noble leisure appropriate to one descended of so high a past and
controlling the future. When he stops affably to
joke with a similarly coffee-and-cream colored
butler of his own old race (who is watering the

The Sublime Passing

Thalhimer's grass betimes, before the heat of the day), and now with that markedly more ebon chauffeur waiting at the door of a Pierce-Arrow for the Strauss family to have done with breakfast, then this bland messenger of the gods holds fanwise across his breast the letters which he has ready to deliver at the Calishes' and the Schwarzschilds' and other of my Nordic neighbors'. When he tucks these letters under his left arm (before the Sycles') it is in order to have both hands free in his retrieving of a magazine which has wedged in the mail pouch. He thus passes out of sight, not to attain our side of the avenue for some while: and I dismiss the naturalistic method of observation in favor of my cooling breakfast.

He, I reflect meanwhile, with rising impatience, is case-hardened; for he does control the future: none the less he stays unperturbed by his responsible mission. There is no telling what interesting nor how financially important letters he may have for me in that soiled yellow mail pouch, and yet he chooses not to deliver them for ever so long. Were the creature humane, were he even fair-minded, he would forthwith cross the street and give me my morning's mail. Instead he passes by with frank unconcern to deliver the morning mail of other persons. Quite unblushingly, so far as vision may plumb, this negroid jack-in-office absconds with my correspondence, in the while that he passes from house to house as the official nuncio of love or death, or of birth or bankruptcy, all in one handful.

Very often, now that June impends, does he announce smilingly the ultimate triumph of romance, in the form of a wedding invitation, but he smiles just as brightly upon the first day of every month when he comes as a realist bearing bills. He affably assigns to each home some dole of joy or of disappointment or of hope or of vexation: he dispenses every known emotion: and there is no house at which he gives his short sharp ring but is made happier or less happy by his coming. Visibly the postman is shaping the fates of my peers and betters in the city tax lists now that he saunters by with his yellow bagful of yet unbestowed knowledge and success and calamity. He comes among us, like the Hours in Theocritus, desired and tardy and bringing with him to all mortals some gift. He, godlike, alone remains unmoved among the changes and the surprises and the perturbations that his advent evokes. It is an august performance upon which I reflect with appropriate emotions and continued impatience.

A considerable while later, well after the morning paper and most of my coffee have been disposed of, I wait in the small Red Room and regard young Nicholas Cabell pendant, in the form of his portrait, over the mantel piece. In that loose fitting, darkly crimson coat, with brass buttons even larger than the postman's buttons, with an infinity of frilled neckcloth in which the laundress has left far too much blueing, and below a looped green velvet curtain such as the eighteenth century found essential to a good likeness—in this guise and posture my forever youthful kinsman has been thinking about what a highly serious matter it is to sit for one's portrait now for a hundred and a half years; and he thus affords me a fine example of perseverance.

Then one hears the grating noise made by the opening of the mail box at our street corner. The postman is removing its contents, and within the instant he will be ringing the front door bell—at his own insufferably long last— with my morning's mail.

6

Vestigia Retrorsum

THROUGH one of those happy turns which keep
matrimony vocal my wife decrees that I should
not answer the postman's ring in person, but
must wait for the butler here to officiate. And
I agree under protest (if she happens still to be
in the house) to this impious arrangement. I
point out that the messenger of fate should be
greeted otherwise than a mere caller: he ought
at the very least, I submit, to be met with trum-
pets and with something fairly elaborate in the
way of genuflexions performed upon the front
porch by the assembled household. There is
none, I explain, that intervenes between the
auctorial home and the almshouse save only
this postman bearing the infrequent cheque:
and we, his dependants, may most wisely accord
him our quotidian deference.

I speak then of *hubris*, recounting its sad fruitage for the race of Laius and of Atreus, of Bourbon and of Hohenzollern. And when I continue with large speculations (very unfavorably received) as to whether upon Judgment Day one should properly wait for Gabriel to send in his card, it is because the two cases do seem to me allied. An author does face judgment, among many other contingencies, whensoever the postman rings. Through the postman alone is an author made acquainted at first hand with the verdicts of that supreme court which is composed of his readers. It is the postman who brings him all the commodious sort of criticism a living author is ever likely to receive, in the form of letters from unknown persons who have been pleased, or perhaps far otherwise affected, by the author's books: and who write to tell him about it with an unbiased honesty such as either prudence or repolishing would stint and recolor in any matter meant to be printed.

Nevertheless one's correspondents do now and then light upon other themes. This morn-

ing I have the normal letter from a girl in normal school, whose English class is studying
modern American authors, and who wishes me
to forward her an account of my life and works.
I have a letter asking how I pronounce my surname, and two letters asking for autographs, and
a letter from a young woman who is staying at
the Hotel William Byrd enclosing the key to
her room, and a letter enclosing twelve slips of
paper for me to write my name on so that my
correspondent can paste these in twelve of my
books. I have letters asking my opinion as to the
standards of English prose style, the vivisection
of dogs, the immortality of the soul, journalism
as an avenue to the pursuit of literature, the
Witches' Sabbat, my philosophy of life, censor-
ship, which one of my books do I like best,
where So-and-So comes into the Branch family
line, how to pronounce my surname, what did
I mean when I wrote such and such a passage
in the Biography of the life of Manuel, whether
love is only an illusion which when it is fulfilled
fades away like a sunset, whether smoking is in-

jurious, how to get into the Society of Colonial Wars, whether I want a secretary, a book which its author is sending me, and how to pronounce my surname.

Apart from all this the postman has brought a letter which cannot be disposed of with the same legerity. It is not an unusual letter, for it says the writer of it is in Richmond for a day or so, at the above address, and hopes to have the pleasure of seeing me at whatsoever hour may be most convenient. It is thus a letter which I have very frequently received without ever detecting either its logic or any civil way of escape.

I in consequence now wish to God that people would let me alone. I remark that I might as well be trying to write in the Capitol Square. I am not, I observe, with a continuance of fine open-and-above-boardness, empowered by the City of Richmond to receive tourists; nor do I think that seeing me comes properly under the heading of pleasure. I submit, to my wife's lack of attention, that I am not lovely to man's eye, nor do I find my conversational gifts especially stimulating to the human mind, and that if people would simply mind their own business! The unsympathizing woman agrees to each of these statements, with a frank lack of interest, in the while that she reads her own letters; and remarks that we can have either anchovies or mussels and some Ravished Virgin cocktails.

Just as the more logical male is about to point out, in not unjustified indignation, that I have already said I am not going to be bothered with the man, just then I notice something in some cloudy fashion familiar about the letter's signature. I recollect that my accursed molestor published, during the last autumn season, a highly promising first novel; and I vote with meek resignation for the mussels. I furthermore deduce I shall have to get this highly promising novel from the Public Library some time to-day and read through enough of its balderdash tonight to be able to talk pleasantly with the young man to-morrow afternoon.

The lady who understands husbands to a degree hardly compatible with unmarred comfort

31

then departs to attend to her household duties out of doors, which include the returning of the key to the young woman at the Hotel William Byrd. But I, prior to going upstairs to express via the typewriter my ecstasy over having to devote an entire afternoon to yet another literary stranger, I fall again to looking at young Nicholas Cabell and to wondering what this other young man may be like.

7

The Recipe for Writers

FOR one I almost always almost enjoy meeting writers. I like, anyhow, their reliability: and I have known in the flesh a great many writers of varying schools and degrees of talent. At one time or another anybody who has ever written anything appears impelled to visit Richmond: and during the last fifteen years I have thus met I know not how many hundred persons with more or less literary credentials. That which they had printed differed immeasurably. Their work displayed nothing in common, and its fruits clearly emanated from unreticently gifted beings whose minds had not anything in common. What pleased and yet puzzled me too was the fact that as private persons—inspirited by the second or third Ravished Virgin, and replete with sandwiches, and seated in the red-

33

covered chair beside my library window,—these writers did all have so very much in common as to convert a conversation with any one of them into a virtually effortless matter.

It were idle to pretend that all the talk made in my library is thus uniformly successful. With the more solid citizenry who now and then get into the room I find social intercourse always to begin unhappily. The trouble is that in their brisk way they take charge of the matter by inquiring, with a soul-chilling sprightliness, whether I am writing anything nowadays? This gambit I admire: I have often planned to adapt it so that I myself might begin talk by demanding, say, of a lawyer whether he as yet retains his practice, of a clergyman whether he is holding any services nowadays, or of a banker whether his bank is still running; but thus far I have not plucked up the requisite élan. I answer, then, that in point of fact I am at work on a book. They ask (with an appreciably sobered geniality, as of one who had hoped for better tidings) what am I going to call it? When I reply that I

34

have not yet decided, the topic of literature appears exhausted; and conversation has to relapse lumberingly into the more fertile fields of Prohibition and the stock market. I suspect that even there it does not scintillate. But I have never found the least trouble in making talk with my fellow writers.

This happy outcome springs from the fact that all the writers whom I have met in the flesh (and for that matter, I daresay, in the looking-glass) have agreed in their large vanity and in their inexplicable jealousy the one of another. These traits are not to be enregistered as cardinal virtues from the point of view of morality, but in social exercise they work out handsomely. That all-engulfing self-conceit (without which no writer, I most firmly believe, can be worth his salt) affords at once a pleasing topic for conversation. I know that the person opposite really does of necessity consider himself a pre-eminent genius—even in my library, with my Collected Works on full view,—and that he requires only to be treated with appropriate deference in the while that we discuss his exploits and revere his books.

The jealousy comes nicely into play the instant that (with the dutifulness of a centurion introducing an Early Christian into the arena) I feed to this lion one or another mention of some other author in terms of artfully mild commendation. The things that a writer can and does very promptly say when any other living writer is tentatively praised continue, even after thirty years of hearing these things, to astonish and delight me. I am spurred to emulousness, and in a while I emule: I draw freely upon my own funds of moral indignation, of superior shruggings, and of derogatory hearsay. There is no possibility of the conversation's languishing until the overrated humbug under discussion is quite disposed of to his very ultimate least frailty and defect. We rejoice, as high-minded artists, that his late book proved a commercial failure: as men of the world, we are not deluded by any exaggerated reports of its actual sales. We know all about it: the poor found-out trickster is on his last legs: and in imagination we glowingly escort him back to the gutter, where he belongs.

Then we revert to talking of my visitor's fine work. By-and-by I feed the visitor the name of yet another contemporary writer. And in this way we get on famously.

I have not ever known this simple program to fail. Now and then I have encountered a literary visitor who declined to deviate for one instant in talk from that visitor's own writings even to vilify the works of others, but such stubborn exceptions are rare, and in any case she keeps on talking. And I attend in contentment, because I have read of how my own dull eyes and drooping eyelids are informed with intelligence only when I am discoursing upon my own books in a fevered monotony of egotism, varied upon the least provocation by shriek after shriek of wounded vanity. One who carries the matter to that extreme must be patient with the likewise afflicted.

In brief, I almost always almost enjoy talking

37

with writers; nor have I gravely held it against them that during my time they have tended toward broad-mindedness as devastatingly as did the clergy. There has been the difference that to my finding the majority of writers have been proselytizing atheists who have viewed with open acerbity my connection with the church of my fathers. The clergy have seemed merely resigned about it. But all my contemporaries in American letters, so near as I can remember, have from the first embraced agnosticism with a deeply religious fervor; they have become zealots of unfaith, very ardently seeking to make converts to all indevotion, and they have seemed to live in an ever-fretful dread of their own not impossible collapse into some form of sectarian belief. In this way and in yet other ways they have convinced me that Americans have not learned in my time to be broad-minded with entire ease, no matter how steadfastly throughout the last fifteen years we of the literati have tried to achieve the urbane union.

38

THE RECIPE FOR WRITERS

Oncoming antiquaries, I suspect, will not ever give us sophisticated writers of the 'twenties our due credit for the pains with which we learned to converse in drawing-rooms about brothels and privies and homosexuality and syphilis and all other affairs which in our first youth were taboo,—and even as yet we who have reached fifty or thereabouts cannot thus discourse, I am afraid, without some visible effort. I have noted a certain paralytic stiffening of the features (such as a wholly willing martyr might, being human, evince at the first sight of his stake) which gave timely warning that the speaker was now about to approach the obscene with genial levity. Even that fine and strong artist who by common consent discourses bawdily with the most natural gusto, him too I have observed a little squeakily to raise his voice in the actual plumping out of each formerly unutterable word whensoever in the presence of ladies he over modestly conveys a general impression of not knowing anybody except bitches and bastards. The effect, in brief, is even here not free, not wholly free, from some visible strain. Yet we stick to it, none the less; and in all such affairs we older writers remain, if anything, rather more untiringly broad-minded than are our juniors, in the same conscientious manner.

8

About Sinning in Season

I FEAR, then, as I consider in what politely ecstatic terms to write this young novelist, that he too may prove a person whom his talents have consecrated to immorality. So many of the visiting literati have fetched with them to Richmond intense and generally queer looking young women, sometimes under the ægis of free love, and sometimes merely as the man's legal wife for the current month, that I too have suffered under the need put upon the creative artist to be fickle and multiversant (and, for choice, priapic) in his amours.

I am so eccentric as to lament this need. That the supreme court to which I have already referred, of the average readers of any author's books, should expect such doings of a fairly successful writer seems fair enough, since it is the

41

comforting salve of the undistinguished citizen to believe that persons of some talked-about achievement, or of superior social station, are at any rate his inferiors morally. My lament is rather that the artist himself is cowed by this superstition and is driven but too often into flat lechery to defend his genius.

I have known far too many male writers who painstakingly honored this creed very much to the hurt of their business in life. Indeed I nowadays look with large wonder upon this onerous superstition and the havoc it has contrived in the doings of innumerable authors whose private affairs are more or less familiar to me,— alluring, as it has done, so many of them to marry indiscriminately and repeatedly; leading them (over and above the time squandered by their broad-mindedness in finding extra-legal bedfellows for their wives) to maintain mistresses long after the age when illicit love-affairs have become a nuisance; affording a robust anthology of fairy tales by stirring up a more than antiquarian interest in the old ways of Sodom;

42

quenching all that quietness which is needed to beget a really fine phrase; and in general forcing the American author who in the least respected his repute as a writer very sedulously to avoid the appearance of any bourgeois virtue at the expense of mere reason.

Nor have our sisters in the scribbling trade denied at any rate their lip service to these hide-bound conventions. Here of course the affair becomes delicate, and I dare accuse no gifted gentlewoman of continence. I merely remark that, although during the last fifteen years I have in private suspected one or two widely known female writers of personal chastity, he would have been a far bolder man than I who durst twit any one of them with such delinquency in the as yet sophisticated state of American letters.

Now here again I think the postman is implicated. Through the postman alone (I reflect once more) is an author kept in touch with inedited public opinion as it quite honestly regards his writing and his personality. How this

43

affair also may speed with women writers I may not presume to say. I say only that day after day the postman brings to every fairly well known male author an invitation to succor one or another misunderstood wife adulterously and to assuage the carnal loneliness of this or the other unattached spinster: if I forbear to speak of those bright young men who desire (as a rule, in violet ink) to enact Antinous to his Hadrian, it is not for lack of subject matter. All these correspondents, then, presuppose the man's sexual piracies so very often, just as an affair of course, that the most unadventurous of penman may well come insensibly to doing that which seems expected of him. In but too many cases this leads to open iniquity such as upsets one's working hours; and after any serious practitioner of the art of writing has mastered his prose style he should be permitted, I think, to live superior to the jogtrot notions of morality.

I would so far honor the conventions that until the man is thirty-five or thereabouts I would bar him from no sort of loose living nor

44

fornication nor crime, remarking only that he will find it more profitable, as a rule, to combine the last-named with an avoidance of the penitentiary. All such depravities, I admit, will later be as grist to the auctorial mill; they will aid to establish his legend; they content his public; and in the long run the books which he writes will not suffer, inasmuch as no prose book written before thirty-five is likely to be of relative importance.

I concede all this. My point is merely that after thirty-five, or by forty at latest, the elect writer has not enough spare time for broad-minded and artistic conduct. He has reached the season wherein, if at all, he must harvest of his baser passions and of his evil doing: even in the teeth of public opinion he may now, I think, avert from sexual immorality with a clear conscience, esteeming it his fairly won privilege to lead that sober and immured life wherein alone he may find full opportunity to pursue his sedentary trade. It has now become his main duty to write, and to give over all to his art, without any further truckling to the vices which his constitution is no longer able to support with distinction. Nor will his fair repute as a writer take hurt from this sobriety, in the last upshot, provided only that his writings survive him; the vicarious lecheries and the mental masturbations of the learned who will edit his remains may be safely counted upon to provide the final years of his biography with the requisite misbehavior.

9

Veils and Emigrants

MEANWHILE it occurs to me that these observations, as to the natural history of prose writers, are perhaps robbed of any large significance by the fact that I may have encountered no authors of profound or enduring worth. About that I of course do not know. For one matter, it has been the fate of my prolonged diversion, in the Biography of the life of Manuel, to fare always an appreciable way apart from the fields wherein my contemporaries were at play: our interests were not ever quite the same: and as one result of this I have very often applauded my confrères with a certain conscious lack of sympathy. I perceived their manifold merits, that is, perforce and with a rather distasteful clarity. There has always been present, just around the corner, the notion that if these so obviously talented persons were selecting their themes and the proper treatment of them with intelligence, then I must be making of myself, in my Poictesmes and my Lichfields, a spectacle which I preferred not to consider.

It has followed—no doubt, as the bitter fruit of this wilding perennial notion—that even nowadays I do not regard any one of my contemporaries quite so seriously as to believe that during my time Shakespeare and the Bible have been hopelessly dispossessed from their rumored supremacy in our literature. None the less do I fear that jealousy may color this verdict: I admit that every current book is unfairly handicapped by its manifest failure to be the book which the publishers describe on the dust jacket: and I know that each era has over modestly believed itself to be bereft of literary genius.

This belief is not wholly due, perhaps, to the polite pretence of every reviewer that the especial author upon whom he is now operating is the reviewer's equal. I suspect the author may be partly to blame, in that he only too often permits his reviewers, and even his potential readers, to see him and to know him personally. He does not with a shrewd humbleness remember that, in the judicious words of Trelawny, "to know an author personally is to destroy the illusion created by his works: if you withdraw the veil of your idol's sanctuary, and see him in his nightcap, you discover a querulous old crone, a sour pedant, a supercilious coxcomb, a servile tuft-hunter, a saucy snob, or, at best, an ordinary mortal."

Edward John Trelawny had known a number of admittedly great authors: and I think that he spoke the truth as to every gifted writer who is yet alive. Living, the writer who has genius gets hourly in the way of his own ability and obscures it. Living, he does but too often, and far too willingly, illustrate what Keats meant by his cryptic saying, "Of all God's creatures a poet is the most unpoetical." Living, he exhibits, not merely in my library but to his beholders at large, that childlike yet that wholly necessary self-conceit and that vivacious jealousy as to

49

which I have spoken: and he in many other ways, and upon every possible occasion, appears at marked pains to stir up surmise as to his mental balance.

Yet every writer of fiction comes among us, let it be remembered, from out of a land in which he is God: he comes from a very high ordaining of love and death and of all human affairs in this more familiar land, which his characters inhabit, to make civil talk for us in our trim drawing-rooms or to foster those more hardy platitudes which alone may flourish upon the bleak lecture platform. We should always remember in our dealings with literary persons that each author is in every essential a foreigner but lately emigrated from the one land which is comprehensible to him; and that also he goes among us perforce in a half-sleep, preserving as best the poor man can the amenities of our physical dreamland by pretending to believe in us. So does he become ludicrous in our eyes because he perceives only too plainly, and cannot for any long while hide his awkward perception, that no one of us is an important or an enduring phenomenon. And about the importance and the enduringness of that world wherein he is God—upon this point also—the deplorable creature may of course be quite right, provided only he has made the grave error of being born a genius.

For this reason I often wonder if ever among these visiting literati I have encountered authentic genius as it went incognito, veiled by the rude requirements of food and pocket money and yet other fleshly foibles. It well may be that this exceedingly boring person, or this seemingly insane person, will figure among the princes and grandees of to-morrow's literature, with a Life and Letters and a very dull host of commentators. The circumstance may even be mentioned, in his Authorized Biography, that on such and such a date he was in Richmond and then visited me, with a footnote to explain who I was. It may be that this young man, to whom I still have not written one line, is that predestined person: and with the eternal sur-

vival of my full name and address (at least, perhaps) thus inexpensively purchasable, I must
by all means answer the young fellow's letter, I
decide, in the traditional large hollow terms of
hospitality.

10

We Revert to Antiquity

I DEFER, I still defer the typing of my false fervors, to reflect that this young man is one of the oncoming generation of American writers, and the season is spring. He will exhibit a respectfulness more suitably reserved for his grandfather, and he will privately regard me with sentiments which I, who recall my attitude toward my own literary elders, prefer not to pry into. He will be troublous to the eye in one way or another: the beginning male author of to-day is but too often suggestive of a slightly crushed fœtus with an insolent mustache. He perhaps will become fervent and oratorical as to some social question about which I know barely and have not any tiniest convictions. He may virtually be counted upon to do a little free-thinking for my benefit in a rather tense young voice. If he does not speak slightingly as to Mr. Hoover, that is, he will at least say something disrespectful about Christ or Miss Willa Cather.

And I in any case shall envy him for the books he thinks he is going to write. Through chance, or through perseverance, or through the more widely recommended medium of filling out a blank form in the corner of an advertisement, it is said, a man may arrive at many desirable stations in this life: but there is no one of them, I am sure, which is quite so desirable as to be a beginning writer in the spring, with preferably every one of your books unwritten.

—Not that the spring season is by any means what it used to be. This morning, for example, is well enough in its own little way, with its fripperies of bright lukewarm sunshine and of baby blue skies and of very pale green leaves and of excited sparrows talking over the nesting problem in the ivy just outside my window. Yet I observe all these latter-day degenerate spring mornings with a pitying calm, for I recollect the incomparable sunshine of more ancient Mays

54

and the demigods who walked (always in couples) among continuous miracles, when everything that happened was unparalleled and so became an abiding memory forever. I recall that youth with its undulled senses penetrates everywhere to an entire world of more delicate sounds and colors and of keener savors, to a world of which the superficial living of mature persons is no longer conscious, I reflect, as I continue to gaze up at the portrait of young Nicholas Cabell; and it occurs to me that the landscape which the artist has indicated beyond the looped green velvet curtain may well be a part of this world.

In point of fact this is probably an idealised version of the young man's estate at Liberty Hall, in Nelson County, Virginia,—as seen, I infer, toward sunset, inasmuch as he would hardly be sitting for his portrait at dawn. There is visible, in any event, a pink sky and under it three modest and unrugged mountains penetrated by an unhurrying river, which then wanders between some six inches of bush-covered

55

banks before being submerged by the battered gilt frame of the picture. The landscape is thus made a terse summarizing of much Virginian mountain scenery, in its gentler aspects; and the landscape might quite as well be a view of the mountains about the Rockbridge Alum Springs, I decide, as of the mountains about Liberty Hall.

For I am now recalling, under the mild thaumaturgy of May, that once upon a time toward the middle of spring, at just this season of May, one used to purchase, with suitably grave consideration, the blue serge suit and the six decisively striped shirts and the shoes with pointed toes and the vivid ties and socks and the balbriggan and the rubber casings needful for a prolonged stay at the Rockbridge Alum. I spent exceedingly many summers there when everybody more or less was as youthful as is this young Nicholas Cabell. And I remember also the Alum as I saw it but a brief while ago fallen away utterly into ruin.

In this outcome the doom of the once magic-haunted place is not, I concede, unique; for all those century-old Virginian mountain resorts which as yet thrived in my youth, howsoever long they were spared by the ruthless wheels of Time's wingéd chariot, were at last crushed by the rubber tires of the automobile. None exists to-day in anything like its former estate. As it once flourished in many cosy and gracious, strange crevices of our Alleghanies and of the Shenandoahs, and appeared here and there in the relatively low Blue Ridge area, the Virginian mountain resort has died, in no least odor of sanctity, among gasoline fumes.

Vacationists, I reflect—with regret that this exceedingly clumsy noun has no synonym,—vacationists now speed from one filling station to another, unrestingly and without trouble, throughout the period of their ever-hurrying freedom: they pause but overnight, or at most for a week-end. When travelling was less facile they journeyed far more slowly, at the start of each summer, toward the Rockbridge Alum (if they were wise) to remain there as long as was

humanly possible: and chance thus brought together some seven or eight hundred strangers
all in temporary detachment from the responsibilities of workaday life, all living together for
a month or so upon terms of light-hearted
promiscuity, in a social ordering such as now
may hardly survive anywhere upon earth.

11

Economy Weighs Its Rewards

I HAVE found it stated (in an advertising pamphlet of the period) that "at the Rockbridge Alum the society is composed of the very cream of the aristocracy of birth and wealth from every section of our country; while not infrequently travelers from distant lands, in search of health and pleasure, find their steps arrested here, and so, held by the charm of untrammelled social intercourse with refined and elegant people, they linger on in this arcadian retreat while the weeks glide into months. Eminent jurists, divines, physicians, statesmen, and successful men of business in every branch of industry, congregate here year after year, giving solidity and a high moral tone to the company; and bringing with them the fair ones of their households, who, by their gentle grace and beauty, are after all the chief attractions of this loveliest of all lovely spots."

That I take to be an account thrice edited—by snobbishness, by caution, and by Southern rhetoric. As near as I recall the matter, the doings of the eminent jurists and the successful men of business and so on (in a most pleasant connivance with the fair ones of the various households) were really not of a nature so exalted as to depress, with solidity and a high moral tone, the assembled company. Yet there is no need nowadays to argue this point, nor any call for me to revive many well-remembered happenings at the Alum which bore upon this exact point—as explicitly, indeed, as when one pops a puffed-up paper bag,—and so I rehash no ancient tittle-tattle. It contents me to remark that if the stage settings were, upon the whole, taken over from Thomas Nelson Page, the comedy, I think, was by Casanova.

All was based upon two very strict social rulings,—first, that the wellbred remained deaf and blind to the conduct of other couples, and, second, that whatever happened at the Alum did not count elsewhere. The waters were reputed to be aphrodisiac, at least to the female: it may be they possessed also some lightly Lethean quality. In any case intimacies flourished, and became tender and passionate, under an ever-present tacit agreement that September was to end all: and September did quite decisively end all, with the curtness of death. You spoke despair, and she became mildly tearful, it might be, when the first red-gum leaves and the sumac began to turn and the number of empty tables in the dining room increased daily: but under these civilities you both accepted without any deep discontent the fact that your mating season was over.

That at least is how I remember it: but I remember too that youth sees all with its own young eyes and has directed them, ever since Cain passed his first summer away from home in the land of Nod, toward pretty much the same goals. It merely happened that my especial land of Nod was called the Rockbridge Alum.

61

So the time sped mighty pleasantly at the Alum when I (like the young novelist to whom I have not yet written that letter, my conscience reminds me) was chargeable with but one published tale or thereabouts; and when, without knowing it, I was gathering material for so many of the tales which were to follow. And to-day the Alum exists but in ruins. I have regarded the place with eyes which are no longer youthful; and all I found there served as a new reminder that the civilization and the ideals of which I was a by-product are now at one with the polity of, let us say, the aforementioned land of Nod.

Here was a dead place, not ever again to be vivified. I saw that the shingled roofs of the red brick cottages had decayed and collapsed inward. The two upper porches of the Central Hotel sagged infirmly; they swayed in a very moderate west wind as I stood there looking up at the theatre of innumerous old escapades, at these avenues of approach to so many rooms which had once every one of them been fur-

nished with straw-bottomed yellow and black-
striped maple-wood chairs and with a yellow and
black-striped double bed and with a yellow and
black-striped bureau upon which a lowered
lamp emitted just enough of sedate yellow light
for you to see by. I reflected that illicit passion
would in my mind always keep a warm odor of
kerosene. Meanwhile it seemed strangely piti-
able that each one of those rooms was as yet ex-
istent, high above me in the air, stripped of all
furnishings, littered with the fallen plaster of
its ceiling, and not ever again to be visited a little after midnight in slippered feet which trod
very cautiously, through the dim long hallways,
over the red and brown matting, and past many
closed dove-colored doors, that had each a number painted on it in fat black figures, until you
had reached the appointed door, which was ajar.

So I went about the Alum alone, noting that
an entire wing of the Grand Hotel had tumbled
down, and that two of the cottages had burned,
and that the Lake House had burned, and that
I now stood in a grassy hollow which had for-

merly been the broad lake's basin. All the wide sloping lawn in front of the Central Hotel was a low jungle of weeds and ragged grass, and three cows were grazing there. They regarded me without interest, unreflectively, as they munched. But I, I remembered the geometrical brown tennis courts, and the trim croquet grounds, and the olive-green card tables set here and there, upon clover leaves and smooth turf, in the shade of these same tall trees, for the diverse pleasuring of the aristocracy of birth and wealth. I remembered how the black bell boys had passed about here nimbly, in their white coats, and how they grinned with yet whiter teeth as they approached you, and how very prancingly they upbore their white-covered oval trays whereupon gleamed in the cool mountain sunlight the frosted amber and the green mint and the submerged red cherry of many juleps. I remembered how upon every afternoon the extremely brass band used to play (for the eminent jurists and the divines and the statesmen and the fair ones who are now grandmothers)

64

the genial music of a recently knighted Arthur
Sullivan and the crashing earlier marches of
Mr. Sousa, in that circular band-stand, painted
a skimmed-milk blue and relieved with touches
of dark crimson, which had utterly vanished
from the centre of this ruined lawn. I remembered many hundreds of my acquaintances who
had once laughed here, and who were now dead.
And it all seemed rather odd as with entire contentment I looked at those three unsympathizing, silent, gaunt, but very broad-bellied cows.

I remembered yet more intimate matters now
that I went about the grounds of this desolate
place with an exceeding contentment. My
youth, as a Latin poet has phrased it, lay buried
under every bush. But the point was that I
viewed all with such contentment as befitted a
well satisfied Economist, because I saw how
much of the Alum had got safely into the eighteen volumes of my book. Up yonder it was that
Townsend kissed Stella; here by this fallen
bridge he had first met Marian Winwood, and
in the water I saw a descendant of those mar-

65

tyred crawfishes with which they over callously amused themselves. The ballroom of the Central Hotel after nightfall would still be, I knew, peculiarly like that Hall of Judgment wherein Jurgen conversed with young Guenevere, for my heart remembered all the ways of the moonlight in that many-windowed, hushed hall. Here was the lawn upon which Jurgen had won back to his never-aging dream of Dorothy la Desirée: over those blue eastward hills (so very like the unrugged small hills behind young Nicholas Cabell) had come Bread and Butter. It was under these great maples that Manuel first encountered Grandfather Death, and through this field of iron weed had blustered the black Serpent of the East. Here, when here curved a gravelled walk way beneath these locust-trees, King Alfgar had died happily under the benefaction of the amused gods of Rorn.

Upon the farther side of Bratton's Run I came again to the path by which Florian de Puysange had ascended to Upper Morven; but me it conducted to the boulder beside which the same Florian had kindled his tiny fire in the gardens of Storisende. The two oddly shaped stones with which he builded his grate were still there. I placed them in their proper position, and for old time's sake I likewise made a little fire of twigs in the impromptu grate, just as Florian had done, in the while that I thought about a vast deal of ancient nonsense.

I could see that all these things had been much pulled about and had been variously improved upon before they got into print. Those other matters which lived in my memory had been similarly transmuted, I could not well doubt, until nothing which I remembered about this place was much like the actual, very faraway happening. Youth had seen everything with eyes to which common matters were not yet grown commonplace, and then memory had refined upon every ecstatic vision, year after year, until my entire past as I had lived it in this place, and as that past yet figured in my mind, had become sheer illusion.

The girls in particular had been thus amia-

bly revised toward perfection. Those deep-bos-
omed, small-waisted goddesses, with hospitable
wide hips, with buoyant coronals of intertwisted
and fluffed hair, whom I believed I had encountered hereabouts (either in gay organdie dresses
which the filmy petticoat, like a frivolous du-
enna, accompanied even to the ankles, or else
in white open-work waists that revealed the
large bows of bright pink or of sky blue ribbon
attached to the superior undergarments), were
each one of them, as I well knew, an exercise in
historical romance just slightly based upon facts.
I virtually had invented all those wondrous beings; and I liked that reflection also, because it
justified me in having used them somewhat
later to make the Biography of the life of
Manuel.

12

Of Yet Further Rewards

I AM interrupted here, as I sit yet looking up at the little country beyond the left shoulder of young Nicholas Cabell, by the sudden strident creaking of the mail box at our street corner. It is the postman bringing me the midday mail before I have typed one untruthful word to the young novelist: and inasmuch as my wife has not yet come in I get to the front door a good while before the butler does.

When I return to the small Red Room I find I have a letter from an admirer who desires me to advance him enough money to go to Europe, where he wishes "to exchange ideas and opinions with H. G. Wells and others." A rabbi in Long Island wants to know how I pronounce my surname. A college student who plans to do a study of my writings for his final thesis in English would like me to instruct my publishers to send him a complimentary set of my books. He needs in particular those volumes issued in limited editions which are now out of print, and he would appreciate my kindness, he adds in a post-script, if I should inscribe each volume for him "not just with a signature, but with an appropriate sentiment," and he would like also a signed photograph. A woman's club wants me to lecture in Buffalo. A newspaper man in California has a bet with a friend as to how I pronounce my surname, and they are asking me to decide the wager. A woman, of unspecified age but matrimonially Jewish, tells me that "breasts and thighs are not all": she is skilled to evoke the more subtle delights of love, she assures me, and she requests one of my book plates. A man of seventy-two wishes me to explain to him sundry references to white pigeons. A schoolboy wants an autograph. A physician, living in Georgia, writes to ask how my surname is pronounced. An obviously young man, as yet ensnared in the net of Greek lechery, wishes to

share with me his Aiëtes, who has a really bril-
liant mind and is six feet tall and uncircumcised.

These letters are in no way a departure from
the daily average (I grieve to reflect), and they
do not matter: but three other letters have come
from at least professedly young women, and
while no one of these either is of any importance, yet they fit in drolly enough with the
drift of my meditations.

The first, a very long document, tells of its
writer's sufferings under phenomena of not infrequent occurrence in the lives of such holy
persons as were St. Hilarion and St. Antony the
Great and St. Margaret of Cortona, in that my
correspondent also is obsessed by demons. The
demands and the doings and the utterances of
these elementals during a single week, she has
recorded here in six closely written large pages.
All that which she has set down deviates from
the lascivious only when it turns to the be-
merded. She sends me her picture; and she is
quite pretty. She wishes to arrange a meeting
with me in Washington, so that she may reveal

to me the true ecstasies of evil. I shall not meet her in Washington.

The second young woman requires my advice as to whether she had better or better not keep her virginity until she marries. "To the body in point," as she quaintly phrases it, with a sort of foreign accent, "there is no particular difficulty in doing this, thanks partly to certain substitute inventions which, to her own feeling at least, are no harm done. I mean, sir, do you suppose that growing older makes a girl glad of her distinction in this regard, and proud to inform her husband, or does it just bring her to regretting her lost opportunities?" She plans to visit an aunt in Richmond next week on her way north, and she will arrange to meet me, so that if I think she is wasting her youth the omission can be remedied. She would prefer, it appears, to begin her amative career in collusion with the author of *The Cream of the Jest*: she says nothing about *Jurgen*, and that pleases me. Nevertheless she will not, I am wholly sure, be successful in arranging our meeting.

OF YET FURTHER REWARDS

My remaining correspondent finds fault with the Biography of the life of Manuel, in that it has depicted "man as a tireless, eternally desirable, and all-satisfying lover." The truth is (she continues) that love-making is one of man's worst failures: and after some pregnant speculations as to the manner in which men continually delude one another concerning this matter, she laments the hypocrisy which various male shortcomings, in the way of amorous technique, impose upon the opposite sex when the oppositeness is literal.

"Of a physiological necessity (she observes) women must make the best of what is offered them. We learn very quickly that the least suggestion of criticism as to the crudity of his bed manners will kindle in any lover a rage of indignation which sends him flying to someone more capable of appreciating the bounties he has to bestow,—and in leaving he casts behind him rankling insults as to the sources of knowledge and the purity of mind of his late companion. We learn that any implication that there

73

is a lack of rhythm, or of poetic feeling, or of imagination, puts even the most practised per-
former into a hysterical tantrum. The mildest
hint that, say, the tempo of the sonata is pref-
erable to that of the *marche militaire* is enough
to thrust him into sulks from which he can be
coaxed only with the most degraded flattery and
with wild pleas that he has wholly misunderstood our delight in his enormousness.

"So we women learn to remember that very
few men really care for women, that only by
rather heroic contortions have they convinced
themselves that they do, and that there is nothing in that caring like the male's pleasure in his
roast beef and his water closet and his clean
linen and in yet other appurtenances of a comfortable existence. We learn to remember that
men are as easily diverted from their pursuit of
women as a little child is from playing with &c.
And above all we remember that, with the ex-
ception of certain cases so rare as to be of doubtful authenticity, men have always put as little
skill and less imagination into their dealings

74

with us than goes into the decoration of a ball for a Knights of Pythias meeting."

After this *cri du cœur* (wherein emotion triumphs quite masterfully over syntax) my correspondent becomes more directly autobiographical. She confesses to many moments of breathless loveliness during her twenty-six years of living. She has been, it appears, flung naked round the head of a lover, from sheer joy, in a summer night's rain—which is of course one way of enjoying yourself if you like it,—she has been appropriated upon an altar especially built for the ceremony, with candles and flowers, she has found the frail pleasures of Lesbos to be poetic and uncloying, and she is contentedly married (with details) to one of the rarest souls on earth. She knows my exact age; and she explains why she counts it in my favor. She suggests that we meet during the next visit I may pay to New York. I shall write her that I hardly ever come to New York.

13

Lads Who Conformed

EACH of these three letters I find in its own way
to be of some interest: but what interests me
much more is for the instant to imagine the exact sentiments with which these letters would
have been read by that beginning novelist who
used to frequent the Alum. He would not have
answered these letters with those sedate safe formulas which I have learned to employ. He
would have answered them all in person, keeping each suggested tryst: and yet he would have
been shocked in, as it were, one compartment
of his mind; for he cherished there, I can now
see, that strange meridional notion of womankind which, none the less, no living Southerner
ever permitted to enter into his practical rela-
tions with any specific woman.

A girl was in theory a superior being, more

modest of thought, more pure of body, and in-
effably more elevated in moral perception, than
a boy might hope to become. Such was the theory nurtured in just one compartment of his
mind. In practice a girl was so much desirable
flesh which protested dutifully, without even
pretending to mean a word of it, in the while
that a boy kissed and touched and investigated,
in a pleasant routine of very gradual approach,
and which by-and-by he gently tilted over, and
accompanied, into recumbency.

All this in no way affected the theory in its
remote small sanctuary; and when he assured
her afterward—in reply to her unvarying question—that he really did respect her just as much
as ever, he spoke truth. He noticed, I remember,
that after that first physical union no girl showed
any regret upon appropriate moral grounds. He
observed that in such intimacies, howsoever
many weeks they lasted, all speech remained inexact and adumbrative. Certain nouns were
avoided, as over explicit; some verbs were so
changed in meaning that "to love" was related

to no one of the various mental states indicated by the dictionary, and "to go" was far dissociated from any idea of departure; to be "sick" did not call for condolence but for relieved congratulations dashed with a little momentary disappointment; whereas the pronouns "I" and "you" and "it" all signified a part of the body. So did it come about that in the bed of a properly brought up young woman, whether single or married, you never heard nor spoke an immodest phrase: that seemed a rule of some instinctive etiquette.

Yet after what was later referred to as "that first time" no girl ever exhibited any least reticence as concerned action. And not merely impassioned action: girls tended, for example, to employ the chamber pot with a frankness which he found inimitable, and flatulence also, he perceived, oppressed them for no long while when once you had become intimate. He used to wonder about these feminine candors tacitly, just as he used to wonder, against his will, about the strange malodors of attained bliss, always quite tacitly. A great number of material phenomena annoyed the young poet; they simply could not be made to fit in with the accepted theory about really nice girls: and yet, somehow, neither these things nor any other things in the least bit affected his rebuffed but firm faith in that theory which was cherished in one compartment of his mind.

It all seems very perplexing—and very far off. It seems perplexing also that this young crimson-coated Nicholas Cabell—so dark and hawk-featured, so serious-minded and yet ardent—who sits forever with his back turned to that little land which is like the Rockbridge Alum, should have come by-and-by to be my great-great-grandfather. One knows that there awaited, when he sat for this portrait, a large deal ahead of him, in the form of military and political doings, and something of prestige, and a handsome but most intimidating wife, and ten white legitimate children, and sad years of lost health, and finally death also. One can imagine him as having just turned away from much footloose nonsense in

79

that little land now forever behind him, to confront these ills and to accept these responsibilities with a gravity which youth alone knows; and for no reason at all allied to logic I esteem it a fact of infinite pathos that my great-great-grandfather—he also—was once so extremely young as this.

—Which brings me roundabout to remembering that to yet other persons does time bring certain responsibilities in this workaday world. So I collect my letters, and I go upstairs to my typewriter preparatory to writing the young novelist after my accustomed formula, and to answering each one of these other letters next Saturday morning after my accustomed formula. There is, I decide, a formula for everything nowadays. No happening seems quite new, and one has for almost every event a tried and dependable recipe. It results that all passes smoothly, without any of youth's fret and wonder and disappointment.

I desire to have nothing changed. Youth does not know the staid, protective, and most strong magic of formulas, I reflect with complete contentment. And I dismiss all thoughts of all very ancient nonsense now that I settle down to applying the correct formulas to these various relics of the postman's short sharp ring.

NEAR A FLAG
IN SUMMER

One of the later schools of the Grecians is at a stand to think what should be in it, that men should love lies; where neither they make for pleasure, as with poets; nor for advantage, as with the merchant, but for the lie's sake. Truth may perhaps come to the price of a pearl, that showeth best by day, but it will not rise to the price of a diamond or carbuncle, that showeth best in varied lights. A mixture of a lie doth ever add pleasure.

14

Deals with Two Above All

AILY to display the Republic's flag, upon a very tall white pole beside the gateway, is the custom of that Virginian summer resort which nowadays (since the demise of the Rockbridge Alum) is best known to my inattentiveness. Inasmuch as Cayford Cottage stands perched a noticeable distance higher than the other buildings at Mountain Lake, it follows that when I sit upon the porch, about my writing, then the flag and I are uplifted to a shared pre-eminence; and through the leisured daylit hours of seven summers we have thus kept each other company, alone in mid-air, at a large remove from the human affairs of earth.

85

It is a most favorable station in which to play
with a portable typewriter and fantasies. No ob-
ligations intrude, nor do any practical affairs
ever climb thus high, like sombre sheriffs, to
arrest me at the suit of common-sense. To the
left hand one may see only an ever-busy and ro-
bustious American flag, and some way beyond
this, the long straight ridge of Salt Pond Mountain, which walls off the eastern horizon with
architectural neatness. I am aware of a far-off,
very lazy jangling of cow-bells at times, or my
consciousness perhaps records, without real conviction, the muffled chugging of a motor car as
it doggedly ascends Doe Mountain, upon which
the flag and I are enthroned. Now and then I
hear the blurred voices of men and women who
are amusing themselves (as unintelligent persons, the philosophic will have noted, quite frequently do) by taking a brisk long walk, at a
reassuring distance away from and beneath me.
But of human affairs there is no visible sign anywhere in that high and bright isolation which
I divide in mid-air with the flag of my country.

Deals with Two Above All

I imagine that the near-by heavens can regard neither of us as an æsthetic success. If I speak without firm conviction it is merely because of one party to this summer-long tête-à-tête I am nowadays an inadequate judge. I have shaved his appearance far too often to appraise it with any interest: but I regard the flag without bias and with relative susceptibility. I regard it perforce whensoever I glance eastward: and this flag flutters intermittently through my thinking.

I note that those seven red stripes and those six white stripes are so alternated as to suggest the uniform of a convict; and this appears to me an illogical arrangement for the flag of a country which began as a partly penal settlement in his British Majesty's Colony of Virginia. I cannot understand why patriotism should thus flaunt to heaven, and proclaim as it were from the housetops, a fact which patriotism must necessarily hush-up upon earth. That blue canton I know to contain some and forty stars; but for seven whole years I have tried without any success to count them, on that ever-moving flag, and thus to discover just how many States there are in the republic which has now and again honored me with an appointment to Federal jury service.

I observe that if the red and white stripes seem a little indiscreet, the blue canton may well reek with irreligion, in that it boldly attempts to improve upon the celestial plan by arranging its own stars in six parallel rows. The effect is more workmanlike perhaps; yet as a communicant of the Protestant Episcopal Church in the United States of America, I am visited by doubts if this re-arrangement be not in rebellion against Article XIV of our faith, which would seem in plain terms to forbid any such supreme work of supererogation as arrogant and impious. I decide to bring up this question whensoever the Bishops, the Clergy, and the Laity, may next be assembled in Convention. I then decide not to. I recollect, in the nick of time, that those some and forty white pentangles were borrowed from the Washington coat-of-arms, in which they did not represent stars but the rowels of spurs, so that when the design is properly understood, no taint of impiety corrupts this flag. There is no conflict between Church and State.

Then I lament in the design of this flag a bleak banishment of the imaginative. The entire affair is mechanical: all is made rigidly, as if with the neat rule of a schoolmaster. This, to be sure, is the trend of all modern flags—to become variously colored problems in plane geometry,—yet I fall to wondering over these new-fangled attempts to compel men to thrill with loyalty toward one or another combination of straight lines and angles. Euclid did not discover patriotism, but only the *pons asinorum*: I prefer to think the two are not exactly synonymous.

This modern habit allows, for one matter, a variousness so narrow as to lead now and then to mere topsy-turvydom. In the event of further hostilities between Belgium and Germany, it occurs to me, each army nowadays would be mustered under the same three black and red and yellow stripes arrayed in a different order.

Equally, should war befall between France and
the Netherlands, all able-bodied freemen upon
both sides would perforce rally, under the stimu-
lus of patriotism and the draft laws, to support
the same flag: whether it were most holy or most
abominable, would depend solely upon whether
this edge or the other were attached to the flag-
staff. The apt corollary, that any virtue may become vicious in a horizontal position, could
hardly be esteemed a good axiom for the nubile
young. Nor would matters be reasonably clarified should Yugoslavia happen to get implicated, entering into battle to assert the moral
superiority of the same red and white and blue
mixture when flown with the blue stripe topmost.

With the symbols of right and wrong thus
plainly interchangeable, it seems possible that
even the Bishops, the Clergy, and the Laity
aforementioned, might be smitten with occasional dim doubts as to the righteousness of cor-
porate arson and homicide *en masse.* . . . But
at this point I desist, before the fidgetings of my

innate piety, from that poor palliative of so much very slatternly writing which is known among virtuosi, they tell me, as the *monologue intérieur*, or as "the stream of consciousness method."

15

Which Defers to Romance

I DESIST from this run of thought because I grant such reflections to be merely rational. They are but such little truths as may frolic piddlingly, as gnats might dance, about yonder large embodiment of a wild and noble fiction. A flag, after all, does very grandly fly in the face of logic to symbolize the honor of a nation. None can define that inconceivable compost of land, and of tradition, and of forests, and of buildings, and of cultural limitations, and of mutually repugnant human beings, and of pandemic prejudice, and of insane legal fictions, and of yet other unrelated odds and ends, which combine to form a "nation." Most of us will encounter somewhat Falstaffian difficulties should we set about any definition of "honor." It follows that if the average man were a creature so abject as to submit to being bullied by his intelligence, he would dismiss these really incomprehensible notions as non-existent: but as it is, he does much better. He reveres and he serves—here as in a great many other instances,—an abstraction which his faculties cannot pretend to grasp, and into the high habitations of which no sort of logic may intrude, after the fashion of a census taker, with blunt questionings.

He elects for this indefensible course: and the flag of his native land, like the weight of his given word and the chastity of his womankind, is kept sacred by his irrational faith. The patriot everywhere, it may be observed, remains always exceedingly careful lest his country's banner become besmirched by any touch of that bloody sponge which is his brain. He very much prefers to find in his heart a deep and awful understanding that whether this or the other stripe be topmost in the flag which a man dies under is, somehow, as important as whether God or the Devil be topmost in the world he is bound for. The flag of every land is thus made a masterwork of

93

romance: and my point is but that it should in its appearance honor duly its creator.

Here the Chinese Empire, for example, displayed a reasonableness which the Chinese Republic did not preserve when the latter dispossessed from the Chinese flag a dragon from out of a fairy tale in favor of a sunrise out of the day's weather report. A sunrise is real; it is even useful: it has no least kinship with any sort of patriotic sentiment. A flag may very properly be emblazoned with a dragon,—or with a tarask, or with a phœnix, or with a salamander, or with any other flamingly irrational monster which, like that wild magnanimity the flag typifies, has existed only in human faith. Yet I do not insist that every national flag should burgeon with just such prodigies. I would merely remark, in confidence, to my fellow patriots, that through our ever-present need to cherish reverently six white stripes and seven red stripes and the tip ends of forty-some spurs, we are being subjected to a considerable strain.

I reflect upon the handsome insignia beneath

which more lucky generations have been as-
sessed and butchered. They pass confusedly
through the back of my mind, in a harlequinade
of glitter and many colors which is a bit ob-
scured by my equal lack of scholarship and of
books of reference during the summer months.
I cannot at all remember what was the national
standard of Chaldea, whereas over the cohorts
of Babylon floated, in so far as goes my ignorance, only that city's well known Hanging Gardens. Yet yonder gleam the twin bulls of Nine-
veh, in their correct military if not especially
warlike posture of running away from each
other. The Egyptians likewise traverse my thinking under a fine medley of fans and of feathers
and of boats and of hawks and of beryl-green
cats. The Dacians deploy stealthily through the
twilight of my confused recollections under a
contorted serpent: the Carians muster there
under a cock. I am aware of the owl of Athens
(which appears to hold in its curved short beak
an olive) and of the seven-colored sphinx of
Thebes. I remember that, until at least the time

95

of Caius Martius, the Romans marched under
five insignia, which depicted severally a wolf, a
horse, a wild boar, a minotaur, and an eagle.
The tribes of Israel also went conspicuously
into battle, I reflect, under such pleasing devices
as scarlet lions and cups of gold and hinds and
oxen and trees and crowned sceptres and asses
and black ships and ears of corn.

Such was the superior taste of antiquity: and
for any one of these heroic standards a liquescent
barber's pole seems a poor substitute. I reflect
likewise that we have all seen red-and-white-
striped peppermint candy so often as to regard
a representation of it, upon howsoever liberal a
scale, with comparative calm. It is a spectacle
which, in itself, connotes rather less of high-
mindedness than of an over-cloying and sticky
saccharinity; and I imagine that in this aspect
it may rhetorically mislead a great many patriotic orators. I wish, in fine, that both the flag
and I were somewhat different looking.

16

"When Freedom from Her Mountain Height ——"

For good or ill, in the while that I write, the national flag of the United States of America remains my ever-present companion and the sole chaperon of my adventures in phrase-shaping. Beyond the flag, as I have said, appears only the unbroken line of one long forest-covered mountain like a large wall. Every tilted acre of this, when I sit down to my writing in June, is steeped with sunlight. The trees are, to my unlearned eyes, indistinguishable in species the one from another at this distance, except that I note the darker green of the hemlocks growing about the foot of Salt Pond Mountain, and I can see also the first chestnut blooms heave and glitter there, like a tremulous Milky Way of more numerously pointed white stars. Above

the flag are the wide heavens, of a less Prussian-
ized blue than is that reorganized firmament in
the canton of the flag; and about these heavens,
now that spring is ending, move unbelievably
large clouds, like the ghosts of dead mountains
in a repentant search of Mahomet.

The flag moves also, but more variously. In
the brisk thin atmosphere it appears outrage-
ously alive. Billows scutter across the flag convulsively from the pole to the outer end and are
flipped rattlingly into the air. The flag collapses and lolls futilely, now to one side, now
another. Then, rampant, it snaps and splutters
as if in extreme moral indignation. It strains furiously to the north. It whips around, with new
vigor, eastward. It jumps and yelps and fawns
about the pole like an excited spaniel. It curls
like the shavings under a carpenter's plane, it
curvets like a restive horse, and it plays at being
a triangular pennant, all in the same moment.
It is irrational and garish and undignified—and
indomitable. This flag in brief stirs up a quite
creditable commotion and a brave rambunc-

tiousness which says, if it says anything, "Look at me! look at me!"

I remark that as the flag moves thus restlessly above the unseen persons whose talking I hear every now and then, so do the heavens move inexorably in their old order above its demented flutterings. No cloud (so far as I have observed) is controlled in its journey by any interstate commerce law; rain, snow and lightning descend in frank disregard of all possible tariff duties; the sun does not pause for an American passport, nor do the stars enter into this flag's dominion in a quota properly determined by Congress. It is almost as though the Kingdom of Heaven had not yet formally recognized the United States of America.

I become for a little while depressed by nature's continued failure to honor my nation, or for that matter the human race, with any least attention. I remember that these so large and impassive skies have seen over-many flags and far too many writers. With all the aforesaid national standards which but recently paraded through my mind, and with some thousands of other national standards, now forever evicted from human reverence into oblivion's scrap-pile and a pedant's occasional mention, I won-der that my friend Mr. John F. Atkins, the night watchman, should think it worth his while to be hoisting this doomed bit of bunting every morning and to be lowering it at sunset pre-cisely. With all those English classics gathering dust upon library shelves, I wonder why any-body should think it worth his while to be writ-ing, as I set about unpacking the portable type-writer. That fellow Shakespeare, for example, has his following of besotted admirers who will say in any case that the man's work is now and then as good as, or even better than, the master-pieces I may tap out this summer. The writings of Milton also will be ranked above mine by many persons who have never read a line of either of our writings: and Chaucer will yet retain his immunity from all fair comparisons, in the impregnability of his Middle English, for months after I have published my next book.

"WHEN FREEDOM &C."

The flag too has touched a moment of weariness. The flag now droops to the farther side of the white pole limply. You would say that a swollen, brightly striped leech with a dark head had toiled to the top of this pole and were clinging there, tired and sated.

17

We Dispose of a Summer

I BEGIN to write. The flag quivers and it con-
torts itself, as yet indecisively. I observe that
Salt Pond Mountain is pockmarked here and
there with that twilight which the taller trees
retain within their foliage. As the June day
grows toward noon, these rounded shadows become elongated into horizontal smudges, and I
wonder without any deep interest what causes
this. The flag lifts sidewise once or twice, very
uncertainly, moving as though with pulses of
senile desire. It droops without attaining erec-
tion. I continue to write.

Now and again one of those large wandering
clouds, only a little way above us, oppresses
some leagues of Salt Pond Mountain with a
scudding continent of darkness, and such parts
of Salt Pond Mountain as stay unobscured are

tinged with a thin wash of gold. Upon these tranquil and clear July mornings (for we have somehow got into July) the green mountain has everywhere a metallic gleaming, which nods and tosses and heaves in the sunlight with a large indolence that I discover to be infectious. At times, when the wind rises, the whole mountain ripples with a multitudinous gray-green flowing, where the under sides of the leaves are exposed.

Billows cross the flag convulsively from the pole to the outer end (or, in preferred technical parlance, so Mr. Atkins informs me, from the hoist to the fly), and they are deported thence with vicious jerks of unmistakably official incivility. I write on and on, with somewhat the staidness of a certified accountant. As July passes (to the ever-audible tapping and lightly tinkling and bumping noise of my typewriter) then the white chestnut blossoms ascend Salt Pond Mountain dispersedly, and they darken to creamy yellow and thence to bronze, and after that the chestnut-trees melt into the prevailing greenness indistinguishably. I continue to write.

The flag becomes fretful: it collapses and it lolls futilely, now to one side, now another. It of a sudden unfurls with violence. It ramps. It snaps and splutters as if in extreme moral indignation. Otherwise there is no change save that with the coming of August, when I am midway in a recopying of my first drafts, the air has become faintly hazed, as though the mountain were viewed through soiled glass. The flag strains furiously to the north. It whips around, with new vigor, eastward, now that the flag and I are visited in our shared isolation by turkey buzzards. These circle and slant and glide about us, and they otherwise disport their obscene bodies with an incredible gracefulness such as would have mightily uplifted the heart of Charles Baudelaire. I pause in my writing when one of them drifts by upon a level with me, so near that I can see the glint of his small, round, and singularly cold eye. The sunlight shines through his extended motionless wings so that

104

they appear pearl-colored and luminous and such as a seraph might use on workdays. He decides I am not yet food for him, and departs with light indolence. I continue to write.

The flag jumps and yelps and fawns about the pole like an excited spaniel. Meanwhile I write in half-drugged absorption, and the same air which sustains the flag with continuous liveliness moves the paper in my typewriter so that it also flaps and crackles.

The chestnut-trees are once more discernible, for a blight has attacked them. This begins, as did the blooming, with the chestnut-trees rooted about the foot of Salt Pond Mountain. One by one these ailing trees emerge from the staid verdancy of the forest as flamboyant lemon-yellow splotches, which, as the leaves die, deepen into brown splotches: then the chestnut-trees just above them on the mountain side are altered in the same way, and the contagion spreads thus visibly to their yet higher kindred. A vagrant and vivid changing in this manner ascends the broad mountain side, dispersedly, all through the latter part of August. I moralize, in an appropriate purpureal prose passage, thus to observe discolored and tattered death going tortuously through the summer woods without ever swerving from the path by which beauty and new life ascended but a month ago when the chestnut-trees were about their blooming. The flag is not interested by my rhetoric. The flag curls like the shavings under a carpenter's plane, it curvets like a restive horse, and it plays at being a triangular pennant.

I continue to write.

I continue to write, and I recopy everything for the third time. Twilight comes earlier now, a good hour earlier than when I began with my writing. My working day is shortened, the air smells of burning brushwood, and it will soon be time to be closing Cayford Cottage for the winter. The bull bat now hunts by day, and the starlings have given up home life: they pass everywhither about Salt Pond Mountain in volatile and disputatious mobs. Otherwise a great calm as of Indian Summer prevails, and the flag droops to the farther side of the white pole. You would say that a swollen, brightly striped leech with a dark head had toiled to the top of this pole and were clinging there, tired and sated.

18

Views an Ambiguous Realm

So is it that throughout the summer I observe
few and unimportant happenings going on eastward, to my left hand, where the flag supervises
every sentence of my writing. So is it too that I
do not often look eastward. When I set about
that daily diversion which for euphony's sake I
describe as my work, I turn well toward the
west, where the vista is otherwise. Westward all
Doe Mountain (to which the northern corner
of Cayford Cottage is more or less firmly attached) sinks away with an abruptness so decisive that the cottage porches jut from the
mountain side very much as shelves project
from a wall. Westward I look across my typewriter keys downward, and always downward,
through naked air. If my privacy be considerable as concerns the east, then occidentally it

attains completeness, inasmuch as the eye can rest upon nothing whatever within the next ten miles westward from the porch railing.

Your gaze reaches, by-and-by, the summit of ancient woods and, still descending toward the remoter side of a broad carpet of moving tree-tops, it finds there a worldwide, extremely far-away country, which appears to be woven of blue smokes and of green mists. Even more than that small land behind young Nicholas Cabell does this country seem familiar. Yonder, I notice, are the forests lying like dark flung-by scarves upon the paler green of cleared fields; yonder are the rivers like narrow shinings; and under the full fall of sunlight a national highway peeps out here and there like the rigid little line of mercury inside a thermometer. Yet further westward all melts bafflingly into a pearl-colored sky without any assured bounds set anywhere between the ends of earth and the beginnings of heaven. The entire vista, in short, is very much as it was when Florian de Puysange gazed down from the high place in Acaire.

Yonder, I am now and then persuaded, lies Poictesme precisely as the province existed in the mid summer of 1723.

Yet I prefer to remain unhidebound topographically. I avoid geographic dogmas, for upon other days the west turns clearer, and out of it lift many flat-topped mountains like a herd of gigantic crocodiles all couched across the west and facing north. About these saurian-shaped mountains move somewhat uncanny clouds, like walls and crags and huge drifting curtains and tall icebergs, like marble cliffs and like complete citadels, because from Cayford Cottage these clouds are seen sidewise, and their astonishing height is thus revealed in a fashion not to be guessed at when you look up at their flat under side from some lower altitude. To the southwest I observe the two hills which have the shaping of a sleeping woman with her hair outspread, just such a pair of hills as Gerald Musgrave saw when he came jauntily to Mispec Moor, and looked down (from the plain comforts of a cottage in many ways not unlike Cayford Cottage) upon the unvisited uplands of Gerald Musgrave's appointed kingdom. Yonder, only a little way to the west, I am now and then persuaded, lies his all-glorious goal precisely as the realm of Antan existed in the mid summer of 1805.

The landmarks are blended so confusingly that one may not say, with any real conviction, from out of just which century this vista survives, nor whether this faraway broad land may be Antan or Poictesme or some yet other magic country. It suggests, for example, Broceliande; it has many points in common with the Forest of Arden; it resembles Avalon; yet there is an assured whiff of El Dorado about it mingled with an undeniable hint of the Hesperides. I in any event regard this dubious and remote large land with exceeding contentment during the pauses of my writing; and it is westward that I look in pursuit of every elusive word or of the smoother turn for a refractory sentence. Meanwhile the flag strains and flaps unseen, but always near to me.

It remains thus out of sight but well within hearing: and this flag's fleet, unflagging, flippity-flop flapping speaks of sturdy and reputable concerns. It reminds me that I am in point of fact looking down upon the commonwealths of Virginia and West Virginia and Kentucky and Tennessee. It recalls the varied industries which thrive there. It speaks of no futile faëry kingdom but of practical affairs—reminding me of the stone-crushing plant and of the new railway bridge which have smartened up Bellegarde, of the excellent filling station where Jurgen formerly lived, and of the electric power plant and the fine steam laundry now operated upon the late site of the Master Philologist's House of Judgment. It speaks of "the American scene," and it urges me (in its more highflown moments) to be "autochthonous."

It twits too. It reminds me of unused knowledge as to the coal mines and the mountaineers down yonder which I have not ever prinked into fiction. It points out that the sincere and ponderable novelist will depict the life in which he has shared, since with this life alone is he familiar; and it adds also a friendly suggestion that such books, with no nonsense about them, sell a great deal better.

It reminds me that the supreme duty of the American writer, as of each foreign notability upon his first visit to our country, is to express a comprehensive and not over flattering opinion as to the present polity and culture of the United States of America. It says, in brief, "Look at me! look at me!" somewhat as I can recall my small son, when at three or thereabouts he had conquered the art of hopping on his left leg, to have cried out over and over again, just as pertinaciously, "Look at me! look at me!"

19

Concerns Practical Matters

No PATRIOT can remain deaf, it is well known,
to the call of his country's flag. So under these
persistent urgings I have now and then wondered for what real reason I have not ever considered, in any one of my writings, some part of
those matters which the flag speaks of. I wonder
why, save for the unimportant and highly ambiguous instance of the first version of *The
Eagle's Shadow* (that tiny comedy which presents people cloistered for a while in the unreal
world of a house-party), I have at no time written any novel which pretended to touch the
known life about me. Even the few stories about
Lichfield which venture some little way into the
present century are painstakingly antedated a
decade or so of years prior to their publication.
The Biography of the life of Manuel could so

easily, so plausibly, and so very profitably, have been extended into the 1920's: and I, in common with the most of my contemporaries in prose, I too could have viewed, with remunerative scornfulness, the American doings of my own muddled and tumultuous era.

Yet I do not wonder about this commercial delinquency with any profound interest. I recognize the many logical reasons which will induce the ambitious writer to avoid handling contemporary life: and I remember I have listed these in another place. But I recognize too that to adopt and to cling to authorship as a profession is in itself an avoidance of every sort of logic. I know that my book has always been to me a diversion, and that the sole aim of my endless typewriting, in all the diverting while I have been about it, has been to divert, before any other person, me. I explain to the flag how I discovered, as far back as in 1916, that when I set about the adding of yet another volume affairs proceeded much more divertingly if I did not attempt to control them.

I would not be thought, I explain also, to be weighing any nonsense about "inspiration." So far as I know, inspiration is a matter, like the phœnix or the salamander, which many have talked about but none has encountered. I mean only that the practised author develops a highly specialized sub-consciousness which decides for him, far more happily than he can do, the theme and the general outline of his writing some while before he sits down at his desk. It tacitly picks out for him, I think, if only he possess the intelligence not to meddle here, such tasks as will be truly and profoundly to his liking. Like a well-trained butler, it brings up from the cellarage of the sub-conscious, without any ostentation, a vintage in all ways suited to the known tastes of the master of the house.

It has never fetched me a contemporaneous American theme in the long while that my familiar has catered to my daily needs with the half-kindly, half-contemptuous tyranny of any other old servant: and if I defer to this arrangement without rejoicing, I defer also without any profitless questions. The knowledge suffices me (as I patiently explain over and yet over again to that ever-impatient flag) that I have never written about contemporary life because —for a reason, or for a concatenation of reasons, as to which I remain contentedly ignorant— that dæmon who in some sort both serves and controls my endless typing does not wish me to write about contemporary life.

This explanation does not content the flag. It still says, "Look at me! look at me!"

But I, to the contrary, I delude myself during these summer days with the improbable notion that there may be a certain inexpensive distinction in not criticizing "the American scene" at a time when no other native prose-writer appears able to avoid this pursuit. It seems to me in my vainglory, as I sit exceedingly high in the brisk air, that a number of my contemporaries have addressed themselves to a theme which is too trivial to be worth writing about when they set to commemorating these United States of America. I can see so very much of earth's sur-

117

face and such appalling profundities of sky that
a mere nation sandwiched somewhere in between the two appears inconsequential. I imagine that the United States of America is but a
transient intruder between the incurious planet
beneath me and yonder incurious heavens. I
think that by-and-by all our America must pass
away, perhaps as Assyria faded into nothingness,
or that perhaps it will be changed as Athens was
changed into a polity which kept only the name
of its earlier self.

I appear to foresee a time when a book based
upon any of our twentieth century *mores* will
be at one with a book dealing with the mercan-
tile code of Sidon, or with the narrow-minded-
ness of village life in Kish during the reign of
Semiramis, or with the regrettable callousness
of that younger generation which took part in
the Second Punic War: and I begin to think
quite affably about the sad surprises which are
in store for my contemporaries.

For the next few centuries or so they may fare
handsomely enough, I concede; but after that

will come the real test, and under it a number of the masterworks most admired by the book-of-the-month clubs will begin to diminish in glory. A book about the United States of America will then deal with over-many affairs which simply will not matter any longer to any living creature: and yet, for all that, those mist-woven lands, entranced forever down yonder, will then not be convulsed with any appropriate sorrow in the form of earthquakes, and that this dreadful sky may not be hung everywhere with mourning banners I am almost certain. Nature will continue in her failure to honor the human race with any least attention.

The childlike fancy arises that it is the assured doom of any serious writing about matters of timely interest to become savorless in a virtual trice (as the Possible Proprietor may reckon the timelessly recurrent affairs of earth and sky) and to rank with those irrelevant sign-posts which I encounter with unconcealed wonder upon the main public highways of Virginia. I read, for example, that "not far from this spot

stood an iron furnace which was destroyed by
the Indians in 1622," or I read that "six miles
east is Raceland, where the racehorse Timoleon
was born in 1814." With every desire to take a
polite interest in the matter, I yet say to myself, "Well, and what of it?"—speaking too under the tweak of a strong suspicion that all my
last year's gasoline taxes may have been squandered by the Highway Commission upon this
very signpost.

To-day then I am temporarily misled into
thinking that, within a thousand or so years,
one may well be voicing much the same question as to a number of those timely and vital
studies of American life which my self-conceded
superiors in judgment are at this moment acclaiming as "autochthonous" masterpieces. It is
but, I know, a passing madness. In my saner
moods I am as ready as anybody else to admit
that the more scornful writers for the better
class reviews, and the members of the Pulitzer
Prize Committees, and all the publishers' pub-
licity men, partake of a shared infallibility: yet

at this precise moment, and from this a little bedizzying height, everything human does appear misleadingly transitory between the implacable old movings of earth and sky.

The flag does not agree to this for one instant. The flag still says, "Look at me! look at me!"

20

Is of Stuff and Nonsense

IN THE while that I write, I am not guided by the flag's long-headed and sound advice. I disregard the flag to an extent which I would not care to discuss with the patriotic daughters of any of our wars: and I look westward when I am writing, toward a land in very little resembling a confluence of four Middle Atlantic States, or any other part of America.

Another sort of flag protects those forests and uplands and wild heaths which are the haunts of all magics. No wonder is strange to it. The refugees from every collapsed mythology have found under the flag of this land a grateful haven: and all those superb bright monsters of which I was thinking just now, as the most fit symbols for patriotism and the other nobler human virtues, have entered into this flag's protection like high-minded expatriates offended by the materialism of scientific research.

It follows that (amid a vegetation which happily blends the very best features of all zones) the fauna of this westward country has become pleasingly various. There one may yet find, I am told, the horned Indian ants which are as large as leopards; there the mantichora (which, it will be recalled, has aspiringly combined the head of an elderly man with the horns of an ox and the feet of a dragon and the stings of four scorpions) consorts with yet other fine zoölogical medleys from out of the Book of Revelation; and there the desert-roving unicorn continues faithfully to worship the Dog Star with sneezes until some virgin or another virgin shall have betrayed him into captivity as lightly as though the monster were only the husband whom she preferred. Upon such commonplace creatures as the chimera, the wyvern, the hydra, the cockatrice, the centaur, and the hippogriffin, here is no need to dwell, I imagine, inasmuch as one must accept these rather as a matter of course in a realm wherein they appear to be no rarer than mares or hunting dogs.

The people who live under this flag are to me a far more grave concern. I may not certainly divine how the inhabitants of a long dead era which labors under the yet further disadvantage of not ever having existed can still retain in this western land an undiminished vitality: but I do know that somehow this has been brought about, through one or another inexplicable outwitting of death and of piety and of common-sense: and whensoever during the last seven summers I have looked westward a few of these people have docilely trooped forth to sit for their portraits.

Kings, princesses and swineherds; abbots, pawnbrokers and wizards; armed champions and tattered beggars and irremediable poets and innumerous witches according to their degrees —all these, along with sundry proconsuls and gods and saints and dukes and a platoon or so of evil or beneficent spirits,—all these have come to me from out of that topsy-turvy west, at one

124

time or another, with an aspect at once wooing and derisive, and seeming very glorious in all the finer colors of sunset. They have rendered me each a frank account of his own improbable doings. They have brought with them love, heroism, wit, loyalty, some humane follies, and a tonic scepticism; they have evoked an interest such as I have not yet invested in my contemporaries nor even in every one of the members of my own family circle; and all these faintly smiling, not wholly human creatures have teased me, now for some seven summers, to bring about their immigration from out of this multicolored province into the black and white pages of the Biography.

They smiled, as I now know, because of my assured inability to manage this: and yet they have not scowled over the one or the other sad parody which I have made of their loveliness whensoever I attempted to obey them. Instead they have returned smilingly, quite as though my huge book did not matter, into their more comely and satisfying everyday life yonder.

They have gone back into that unique land desired by all poets in which one may live with
more competence; in which every least action is
high-heartedly rounded off with the right ges-
ture and with wholly adequate talking; and into
which no one of our terrene shortcomings, in
the way of timid vice or of stinted virtue, may
ever intrude any shabbiness. They have forgotten me and my tinkling typewriter, in brief,
very lightly, without fretting over the carica-
tures which I have made of their elfin splendors
so laboriously: and I too have put these elusive
shining people out of mind, for my own comfort's sake, now that another tale about "men
as they ought to be" has been botched through
somehow to its last bungled paragraph.

I dismiss them with fair equanimity, because
at bottom I am no more eager to follow after
these glittering persons into their remote land
than was Duke Prospero to return to his Island.
Like him, I find that common-sense prefers my
accustomed snug home, in which I may abide
with contentment. Yet I am pleasurably visited

now and then by the irrationalities of a poetic turn of mind—and by a folly which finds the old incongruity between the dream and the accomplishment a rather heartbreaking business; and to which that half-revealed land remains tauntingly unattainable; and which continues to prefer these not wholly human people to my contemporaries.

So does it come about that at Cayford Cottage when I play with a portable typewriter, in complete contentment, I sit with my back turned to the ever-busy flag of my native republic, and that I look westward toward the unique land which these people inhabit. I then believe—at least temporarily—that all which my heart desires happens instantly in this lovely land; I believe that my bankrupt dreams all prosper in this faraway country radiantly; and I believe too that upon the national flag which waves over all its unseen towns and fortresses (wherein nonsense reigns, wherein beauty yet endures) one would discover ramping a silver stallion.

BEFORE ÆSRED
IN AUTUMN

Amidst the gallantry and misery of the world; jollity, pride, perplexities and cares, simplicity and villany; subtlety, knavery, candor and integrity, mutually mixed and offering themselves, I rub on "privus privatus"; as I have still lived, so I now continue: saving that sometimes, as Diogenes went into the city, and Democritus to the haven, I did walk abroad, and could not choose but make some little observations.

21

Speaks of Nero's Legacy

ITH the coming of autumn, and with our return homeward (to that city which when indicated as Richmond-in-Virginia has successfully irritated so very many persons whose opprobrium seemed desirable), then I exchange that summer-long comradeship of the American flag for an influence at least equally favorable to creative writing. With the coming of autumn, then once again I divert myself in the little black and silver room wherein, between breakfast- and supper-time, I play face to face with pallid Æsred,—who is of course Our Lady of Compromise and of Conformity, and the inveterate mistress of all middle ways.

This arrangement involves no supernal dealings. The all-ruling goddess does not honor me unworthy with any personal intimacy such as, in the Homeric phrase, fair-tressed Demeter very disastrously accorded to Iasion in the thrice-ploughed fallow field. I mean only that throughout the season when I am typing in the little black and silver room Æsred is to be seen always, but merely, in the bleak form of that heroic-size bust which Edmond Amateis hewed in her likeness from a block of Greek marble that was imported to Rome during the first century of our era, to be used in the construction of Nero's Golden House,—and which some nineteen centuries later was unearthed by a building contractor while digging the foundations of a modern building on Mons Esquilinus, and so came by-and-by, through the accomplished hands of Mr. Amateis, into my keeping.

It is pleasing, I find, that a bit of Nero's property should to-day be my property. The fact appears to establish a direct link, howsoever tenuous, between young ruddy Nero and that

gray person who is just now tapping out this
paragraph upon my typewriter. It is pleasing to
reflect that Æsred also, when embryonic in
marble, was once subservient, as in those days
for the only time in history the entire civilized
world was subservient, throughout the turbu-
lent length of thirteen years, to the rule of an
artist, and of a red-headed artist at that. Yet I
do not believe Æsred thinks about this con-
tributory evidence as to the unluckiness of thirteen now that she stands opposite my desk and
looks at me with inexact attention, incuriously,
with vague eyes. The block of marble has become the head and throat of a pale giantess who
has doubtless her own thoughts: but I question
if they often hark back, in the morose indignation with which very practical persons regard
any sort of ecstasy, to the Golden House and to
the over-fervent doings there in that remote
time when Æsred was at the disposal of a feath-
erbrained poet who could not be counted on to
do that which his neighbors expected. It was a
quite unsettling experience; but Æsred has

more important matters to consider nowadays: and among these important matters, one infers, I am not included.

Me now, in place of Nero, is the plump and slightly sullen goddess compelled to observe without sympathy. She and I have the little room to ourselves, and at no moment am I wholly released from the knowledge that she is watching my antics. Her disapproval of them is unflavored with any bitterness because her contempt for me is complete. It is her divine opinion this afternoon that I smoke too many cigarettes for the good of my after all quite negligible health; and that I fidget and writhe about in my swivel chair (of which, I feel, she resents the recurrent creaking) to an extent past the normal endurance of the human buttock; and that I far too often neglect my trivial trade in order to look, through a rain-flecked window pane, at nothing more grave and weighty than are the ruined reds of those drenched October oak-trees and, rising beyond them, the gray tower of the Hotel William Byrd.

Of this multiform disapproval I am continually conscious. As I bend over the desk about my writing, I am crouched before Æsred in something rather like an attitude of supplication: whensoever I look up from the typewriter keys, and over the top of my reading glasses so that I may quite clearly see my chaperon, I fidget yet a little more under her calm but uncordial gaze. Æsred still remembers that foiled poet, Nero Claudius Cæsar, I infer: she has not forgotten that of which a writer is capable when no restraints in the way of time-serving or of expediency impede his desires.

But, even so, Æsred has far more important matters to consider nowadays. She does not deeply bother about me, either one way or another: she allows the clarity of my insignificance to rank as a palliative to the offensiveness of my folly.

22

A Lady in Several Aspects

OF THAT place which Æsred holds in the
mythology of Poictesme much has been said
elsewhere. She appears sometimes as a very aged
person with her head wrapped in a kitchen
towel: in this avatar she was known to Jurgen
as Sereda, the controller of Wednesdays and of
whatsoever is blue in this world, and as an untiring bleacher who takes the color and the fine
vigor out of all things. But in a different aspect
the goddess became visible as the bust shows
her; she was thus encountered at her snug home
upon Mispec Moor, by Madoc and by Gerald
Musgrave and by yet other persons, as a woman
in the full prime of life, wearing that queer
crown from which were copied later the four
suits in a pack of playing cards: and she was
known then as Æsred, or as Maya of the Fair

Breasts. In this more comely manifestation she figures as the beneficent witch who transforms men into domestic animals, and who withholds them lovingly from the dangers of thought and of too high endeavor. She is thus represented in the bust before me,—not as Sereda but as Æsred.

It is probable (says Bülg) that Æsred was in the beginning an Earth goddess, allied to Demeter and Erda and Isis. All these were viewed, the learned will remember, as Earth the All-Mother, who bears and nourishes mankind. In the later cult of Æsred this conception of Earth is refined upon with a shift of emphasis, and Earth becomes rather the All-Wife. Man, in brief, is wedded to Earth inseparably, and the ever-present union of spirit and matter is prefigured as a marriage terminable by death alone.

Bülg expands handsomely upon this truism; and he has made of Æsred, before his rhetoric has done with her, a figure far more vast. She becomes under his ardent handling a symbol of all earth's civilization, which for its continuance

137

depends upon those mutual agreements and those compromises through which every individual householder, no matter what nor how esoteric may be the field of his daily labor, yet has this much in common with all his fellow citizens, that the employment of each is fixed and fore-announced. I mean, for example, that under the amenities of civilized life the plumber is not free to set up as a dentist to-morrow morning, nor may any bishop become, just upon the spur of the moment, a judge in the circuit court. Instead, each one of the four will by ordinary continue to do that which is expected of him; and in this way he will remain a more or less useful, because a predictable, part of human society.

Such is Bülg's interpretation. But I prefer, for the present, to regard the old legend in its least elaborate form, that form in which Æsred stays simply the lady who without argument or protest makes the best of things as they immediately are. Dwelling in unassuming comfort within sight of that Antan which is the goal of all the gods of men, and the goal too of all poets, she has no faintest desire to travel thither at a hazard of her accustomed way of living; and she sees to it that her husbands also refrain from any such ambiguous bargain. Poets alone of restive male persons Æsred may not always detain upon Mispec Moor: she does not traffic in that sustenance, or in that drug it may be, which their natures require: so a great many of these unfortunates fare scornfully beyond her, toward Antan. All other men, though, Æsred does detain at last, without much exertion; and she holds them entranced by the most wholesome sort of contentment until each one of these mortal men has said to himself, frankly, in his own heart:

"What need have I to be seeking unfamiliar places so that I may rule over them? That way is troubled, and too full of noise and striving. It is better to be content. It is better to be content with the dear, common happenings of human life, shared loyally with the one woman whose love for me is limitless and does not change, for all that it is blind to none of my failings. It is the part of wisdom to know that these things are enough and very far beyond my deserts. It is the part of an honest husband not ever to be insanely hankering after any more high-hearted manner of living, which is out of my reach, or, at any rate, is attained through more trouble than it is probably worth. And in the cordial glow of his own hearth-fire each one of us discovers by-and-by that the middle way of life is best."

When once the quelled wayfarer has said that, then Æsred's task is done. She has made the man respectable.

23

Some Who Blaspheme

IN THE mythology of Poictesme there was, save only Koshchei the Deathless, none more mighty than Æsred, Our Lady of Compromise. And her reign endures, for all that so many of the pagan immortals had a poor time of it when Christianity triumphed. Heine and Pater and Swinburne and Arthur Machen and Lord Dunsany and Saki, and I may not tell how many other writers, have recorded their charming and cruel tales of how these bankrupt gods, "when bereft alike of shelter and ambrosia," continued to go furtively about earth upon treacherous errands; preserving always a subtle and malign grace and some fragment of ruined power; using unhallowed means to incite, where honor was denied to their fallen godhead, a fevered carnality; and requiting any human compliance thereto with fatal caresses. Whatsoever of their other traits had become enervated and beclouded, yet the favors of these once celestial beings remained deadly; so that long after Golgotha their smiling continued to work human ruin just as inevitably as when fair-tressed Demeter smiled upon Iasion in the thrice-ploughed fallow field, and lightnings consumed the mortal man in the instant that his life enrapturedly went out of him, into the womb of a goddess.

—All which is quite the approved style wherein to handle this theme, and employs with discretion the dear old decadent phrasing, I observe complacently. I dismiss with frank fondness the impassioned mincings of the true æsthete, and I continue my reflections in cadences a bit less preciously foreplanned.

I reflect that Æsred, the eternal conformist, the untiring contriver of compromise, and the lady who makes the best of things as they immediately are, if she lost a follower or two in the first flush of Christianity, regained them all at the moment Christianity became respectable and worthy of her patronage. The power of Our Lady of Conformity endures to-day—I remember, as I look up at the indomitable, gross features of Æsred—more strong than it has ever been. She teaches still—as clearly at Richmond-in-Virginia as upon Mispec Moor—that all extremes are unwise. She allures us for our own good to do that which is expected. She fosters that strange common-sense which is feminine; and she persuades a number of male creatures to obey the dictates of this common-sense.

Æsred, I take it, is that spirit of mediocrity which human experience has shown to be the most profitable guide for mankind in every department of living. She was once, in Carlyle's fine but now obsolete term, gigmanity: since motor cars prevailed she has become, so near as one may phrase it, respectability; and Codman indeed has described her as the Mrs. Grundy of the immortals. Yet in a wider sense, I recall, just as Bülg has pointed out, she embodies all human civilization, which can function only

143

through each man's doing that predictable thing which is expected of him. This Æsred is, I decide,—in the one word which sums up everything—conformity.

It has followed that many poets have taken the field against Æsred ever since, some 460 years before our era, Æschylus first introduced into his *Prometheus Bound* a curt and acid-etched portrait of the conformist in the rôle of the trimming Titan Oceanus. Indeed the considerate may very well grieve to observe the steadfastness with which a large number of creative writers have assailed and derided the respectable tenets of their time; and the poets, they in especial, have inclined from the first to dwell over-zestfully upon the double-dealings connected with being a well-thought-of citizen. It has not contented a majority of the poets to go beyond Æsred and to refuse the comforts of her snug ways and domains: only too many of these wastrels have delayed long enough in their passing to chalk up extreme opprobrium upon the neat walls they refused to enter.

Some Who Blaspheme

This fashion of overt denunciation (as opposed to the comparative restraint of Æschylus) was begun perhaps by that very fine poet Christ in his handling of the Scribes and Pharisees; and in this single respect He has not ever lacked whole-hearted followers. It has been noted by many of us, no doubt, that only the other day Mr. Sinclair Lewis handled the Rev. Elmer Gantry in somewhat the same manner.

As a person of hazardous education, I briefly confine my regard to the literature of English-speaking peoples (upon the understanding that, even though for a while they have ceased to produce literature, the British yet speak English of a sort) —and I find no theme to be more frequent in this literature than is the unmasking of some respectable conformist to all the better-thought-of ideals. It is not needful to emphasize those pious-spoken and lecherous friars and clerks and monks whom Chaucer translated from Italian sources into a mediæval jargon which is now but little less illegible than Coptic. I begin where actual English begins, and I remark that all Elizabethan and Jacobean literature pullulates with puritanic persons so very unequivocally christened as were Zeal-of-the-Land Busy and Giles Overreach and Luke Frugal and Tribulation Wholesome and Languebeau Snuffe and yet other superficial models of integrity,—a spawning of small souls to which Shakespeare duly contributed, in the rôles of Malvolio and of Angelo.

To these bulwarks of respectability succeeded in public derision the Gripes and Maskwells and Vernishes and Fainalls and Moneytraps of Restoration comedy. Swift afterward had his full say as to the better-thought-of bulwarks of Queen Anne's and the first Georges' polity. Then Fielding introduced into the English novel, at the moment of its inception, Blifil: and with that the hunt was up, full-cry, in a field wherein it has never flagged.

I at the moment can think of hardly any standard English novel which has not unmasked at least one over-respectable double-dealer since Thackeray fell afoul of snobbishness in some twenty-six volumes, and Dickens took up the life-long crusade which began with Stiggins as a target and progressed, by way of Pecksniff and Heep and Chadband, to Luke Honeythunder. Here is an obsession common to Mark Twain, Dante and Jane Austen. Here is the perhaps unique tie which unites George Meredith with Bulwer Lytton, and Oscar Wilde with Theodore Dreiser, and H. L. Mencken with Charlotte Brontë. Everywhere I detect writers of every degree pointing out, with unexplained animosity, and (as the centuries pass) with a noticeable effect of reiteration, that the habitual conformist can be neither candid nor rational.

24

As to Living in Glass Houses

I AM afraid, upon this gray and dank October afternoon, that the professional writer does not consider often enough his own abstensions from candor and rationality. There is a great deal which needs to be said, and which thus far has lacked utterance, about the hypocrisy and the self-deceit that must necessarily, in a world ruled by Æsred, sustain every artist and in particular the creative writer. I am not considering here the popular novelist who is sustained far more intelligently by the proceeds from the sale of his books,—and who remains in any event inconsiderable. I am thinking of the writer who approaches his art seriously, with an hypocrisy which is in some sort holy and with a self-deceit that is sane, when he asserts, and in many instances persuades himself, that the influence of books is of profound and wide significance. He assumes in short that the man who writes a book may be about a task which really and even gravely matters: and he finds too among the ill-balanced and the dull-witted a great many persons who accept this tenet amicably.

For myself, I observe, with quite honest regret, that when once we revert to honest thinking we find this fallacy explodes in whatever a jiffy may happen to be, and reveals all literary values to be mostly humbug. I hasten to add that no writer may concede this fact with any possible profit. As Isabel Paterson has well said, what a writer most needs is a kindly conspiracy to take him seriously; and to foster this conspiracy in his own thinking is the man's primal duty toward his art.

Here his hypocrisy is holy, and his self-deceit becomes sane, in that no other tools are at hand to serve a cause which appears to him supremely exalted. The misled creature, will he or will he not, is an artist: and he must in one way or another contrive to delude himself, throughout at

149

least the time of his powers' growth and full-
ness, as to the gravity of his folderol. He must
manage to believe, somehow, that the book he
labors on is an important enterprise: and he
must resolutely keep out of mind the truth that
to no other one human being can it ever be
important for any ponderable while. It is gratifying to note that, so naïve is the artist's temperament, this self-deception may be maintained
for years hand-running, and it evaporates in
some cases only with the last dim view of the
family physician as he administers the oxygen.

Still, one touches here, I think, yet another
explanation of the fact that many writers fall
away, with advancing age, into a decrease of
forcefulness, after their powers of reason have
increased beyond the modest limits suited to the
creative artist, and late middle life, with its uncivil ally experience, has brought the assured
knowledge that every author is perforce about
rather trivial ends. He writes well or he writes
badly: either way, it does not actually matter.
The book upon which he is at labor may per-

haps live for a long while after he has been valeted by the mortician, yet although his book should reach to the span of Old Parr, or even to that of Methuselah, it will furthermore resemble these patriarchs by achieving during a prolonged existence nothing of any importance.

Upon this gray October afternoon, as I consider the unimpressionable pale giantess who confronts me, I am of the opinion (which I trust to change upon the very next sunny day) that books are of grave weight in the life of no reader, and that at best they fill a small space in it haphazardly. No virile male has ever left a personable and fairly compliant woman for Homer, I observe low-spiritedly; we do not forget a toothache through Shakespeare's most artful charming, nor is there any known book so excellent as to detain the sane householder for one instant after he has heard the announcement of dinner. In the seraglio of the wise man literature is an odalisque, but hardly the head wife; nor does the artist who purveys this casual lady of the evening remain exempt from mono-syllabic description.

This much at least, it seems to a temporarily dejected me, must every mature author per-ceive, by-and-by, in the while that his junior rivals talk about the dignity of their art with a lack of candor and of rationality such as not many molders of general opinion in Congress or in pulpits habitually surpass. These rather charming, very zealous young writers of remain-dered novels, it appears to me, a little too vio-lently assail the over respectable for lacking just the two virtues in which the sincere creative artist can never indulge. But all is proverbially fair, I reflect, in war: and the romanticists who as yet retain the summer of their strength wage against Æsred and the sober cohorts of Æsred an eternal rebellion of which the outcome does not vary.

25

The Homage of Wisdom

VERY great is this Æsred who teaches all to conform the one with another. She embodies that
mediocrity which is sublime, if it indeed be not
omnipotent. She is served by the most powerful,
even as Tamburlaine was served by kings. The
high remain exalted only at her sufferance: all
that upon which she looks coldly must perish.
Bank presidents run eagerly before her, as the
heralds of Æsred: schoolmasters are her janis-
saries: the law is the bearer of her bow-string:
and legislative assemblies dance corybantically
in her train. She is attended also by the police,
and the clergy of all accepted faiths march at her
side crying out, Conform!

Great and exceedingly great is this Æsred
who has summoned our blest kind from the
jungle and from that independence which the

beasts preserve brutally. One tribe of apes, and one tribe alone, she has tutored to do at all times that which seemed expected. With one magic, and a very little magic, she has builded up interminable proud cities, street upon serried street; has sent armies blaring about the world's flanks, and has caused airplanes to tumble from the clouds; has fashioned cuff-buttons and cathedrals and contraceptives, showing us the new comfort to be got of each; has made of the heaven-born lightnings our lackeys that needs scamper without any dignity along small wires, and traffic humbly among sewers, to discharge our common affairs; has fetched us tea from China, and coffee from out of Arabia, and poison from the bootlegger; has likewise made our lips familiar with hypocrisy and vainglory; and has rooted very deep a large dread of our fellows' disfavor in every human heart. She has, in brief, civilized us: the enlightened nations march at the side of Æsred crying out, Conform!

All they among mankind who, in a manner of speaking, are rational, all these perceive that

The Homage of Wisdom

Æsred has wisdom. She proclaims that which it is good for every man to believe. Her wisdom may be rule of thumb; yet it serves handsomely. She has but one commandment for her courtiers, Do that which seems expected: upon her servitors she has put but one refrainment, Thou shalt not offend against the notions of thy neighbor. There are in her code no complexities. Yet this lean code may well serve to purchase a quiet living in the perilous while between a man's birth and his death. It serves very often to purchase shining station and a complacent address: it conducts many toward a figuring out of large surtaxes on or before the fifteenth of every March: it has led to the White House: and it has secured for sundry of its devotees the final tribute which any man may hope for upon earth, of having a picture of his funeral in the rotogravure sections. Such blessings may the faithful obtain because the wisdom of Æsred is a pragmatic wisdom; it is not toplofty; it remains always, as one might say, epigeal: and she prompts adherence to "that which is accustomed, that which holds in familiar usage," not as an entirely satisfactory program for human living, but as by long odds the best working program which the busied generations, through trial and error, have yet devised. All who are wise march at the side of Æsred crying out, Conform!

She has her æsthetics, too, and her valiant servitors no less than her strident defamers in every field of literature. It is customary, I know, to deride those books which evince a high moral tone over-liberally sugared, those peaceful books which the untroubled by literary talent purvey tranquilly for the immature-minded of all ages. I would not defend such books, beyond admitting that their liberal earnings support the American publisher, and thus enable him to bring out an occasional volume which displays genius at a fair monetary loss. I reflect also that true mediocrity works now and then in other media more stably. It was Æsred, I think, who blazed the not uncelebrated *meden agan* which was the pathway of all Greek art during

156

the period of that art's mature vigor. It was Æsred who inspired the most wise and the most durable of human poets, Horace. She contributed at least the books of the Proverbs and of Psalms to the Bible, and she dictated to Shakespeare all his more popular quotations. And it was Æsred who stood always at the elbow of Molière when he was writing his comedies.

That is a thought which prompts me to look with quite real respect toward Our Lady of Conformity; and I become well satisfied to write under a patronship so august. "La parfaite raison, madame," I remark ingratiatingly, "fuit toute extrémité; et veut que l'on soit sage avec sobriété."

She remains remarkably marble to my advances. Nor do any shrill dissenters incommode her, either, when exceptious ink-stained romanticists cry out against the narcotics of conformity. Books may not trouble any clear-headed being's strong preference for the safe, because foreknown, and the soundly builded ways of respectability,—the time-approved ways, in brief, of "that which is accustomed, that which holds in familiar usage."

Into my meditations at this point enters the authoress of *Uncle Tom's Cabin* upon the incongruous arm of Jean Jacques Rousseau: for I recall it is yet said that a book may precipitate a civil war or a revolution. I think the statement is open to doubt. I venture to be perfectly certain that no book can affect human nature. The mass of men desire security and a knowledge of what to expect upon at least this side of the grave: they must purchase this perforce in the one way that has thus far been discovered, by each man's doing that which is expected of him. Here the clichés of fate combine with the cowardice of human nature irresistibly: and so does wise Æsred even to-day retain her power and still convert men into domestic animals just as of old.

26

That Which Endures

AGAINST wise Æsred generation after generation
of young romanticists has gone into shrill-voiced
revolt. With indignation and with manifestoes
and with the very loftiest motives they have
marched up against Æsred under a barrage of
fulminating books and explosive small magazines. They have exposed that which they
sweepingly called "the truth" about marriage
and high finance and politics and church members and all the other adjuncts of respectability.
Yet by-and-by these scribbling zealots pass, tacit
now and outworn: and the spate of their verbi-
age has availed nothing. Æsred endures. She
notes perhaps that a new lot of those young people are to-day in uproar against her. That does
not matter to wise Æsred, who perceives that
books are only books; who knows that for man-

kind all truth is unknowable; and who answers
serenely, alike to the shouting of these rebels
and to the invocation of her courtiers. Do that
which seems expected, and do not offend against
the notions of thy neighbor.

So I esteem it wholesome to write as a postu-
lant before Æsred. As the flag in summer, so
now in the year's autumn does this bust keep
me in mind of ideals which I may respect without of necessity sharing. I at least have not ever
wittingly offended Æsred. Throughout the last
some and twenty years, in the while that my
more temerarious fellows have with untiring
typewriters assailed and derided her notions, I
have written on sedately in praise of monogamy
in *Jurgen*, and of keeping up appearances in
Figures of Earth, and of chastity in *Something
About Eve*, and of moderation in *The High
Place*, and of womanhood in *Domnei*, and of
religion in *The Silver Stallion*: and indeed
throughout the long building of the Biography
I have at every instant upheld, in my own un-
presuming way, all that Æsred endorses as the

more comfortable fetishes for a man to believe in.

Besides, as I grow older, I find I am more than usual calm (without exactly completing Pet Marjorie's phrase) as to all questions of large social import. I burn with generous indignation over this world's pig-headedness and injustice at no time whatever. I perceive, contrariwise, the practice of a sedate pessimism to be a firm savior of contentment, and the constant purveyor of some pleasure-giving surprise when, as happens daily, this or the other affair turns out perceptibly less ill than I had looked for. I do not expect anyone to be intelligent or large-hearted: and my fellows therefore delight me by revealing unsuspected virtues or else justify my clear-sightedness, in an even more gratifying fashion. So do I remain well content to recognize that a not unwholesome sort of dullness and a hand-to-mouth compromising with reality do in the long run rule the material world and upon the whole pilot it acceptably. So am I moved to no carping against Æsred,

who—once more, upon the whole—has dealt
with me not unkindly.

I regard this world of hers which I inhabit
under her sufferance, and that which I see demands no enthusiastic approval: but it does not
vitally interest me, who have, after all, my writing to play with. It very certainly does not en-
rage me to the right pitch of the radical
weeklies, for I perceive that under Æsred's no
doubt dunderheaded ruling the lot of a creative writer is favored. His vocation, as I reflected
but now, may well be trivial: yet is he paid for
the performing of it, with a great largesse. For,
lo! the weakling sits alone and makes quite
small marks upon paper, and these marks become magical, bedrugging him. It matters no
bean's worth if he be a heavy dunce, or a light
simpleton, about the composing of mere balderdash and drivel: the magic he has evoked takes
a friendly care of that, and its art preserves him
in his own belief as a strong thaumaturgist
about the working of ever-living prodigies. The
æs perennius perhaps deficient from his com-

pleted book is thus not ever lacking from an author's self-conceit in the time when he is writing his book.

What indeed has he in that hour to be modest about? All wisdom attends him docilely, and through his spacious mind frisk the most killing witticisms. Beauty repairs to him, come smilingly from out of her sovran shrine, with such an agile hastiness that all her customary veils have been forgotten. Truth woos him in the same frank nakedness; urbanity guides his progress with never any misstep; immortality beckons; and quite perfect phrases pop out of nowhere into his complacent attention. He is uplift a great way beyond mankind: he regards that lesser race with affability, with divine derision, and with a complete understanding, in the while that he embalms, for ever, his pick of them in the miraculous spicery of his picked words. He becomes, in brief, a god about the making of his own world after his own sheer whim, and about the colonizing of this world with many thrice-lucky inhabitants who enjoy the supreme honor of having been created in his likeness.

I mean, of course, that is how it seems to the drugged scalawag in the time when he is writing. Sometimes his book is really not quite so good as all that comes to. My point, though, is that in Æsred's world he is permitted to taste these high and abnormal joys, and to induce these sublime trances, under the shallow pretext of working for his living. My point is that he now and then does actually earn his material support by his indulgence in just these ecstasies. My point is that in a world wherein all other drug addicts are frowned on, are pestered with wise advice and physicians, and are locked up in asylums, the creative writer is left unmolested.

That his tribe, of all tribes, should attack Æsred, who permits and who even condescendingly fosters this unparalleled favoritism, appears to me a distasteful flowering of ingratitude: and toward it I at least shall contribute no petal. I prefer with polite self-effacement to

164

speak no evil whatever against a scheme by which I profit thus directly. I am conscious of no tiniest hankering to expose or to denounce, nor in fact to alter, any of Æsred's arrangements. To the pursuers of my especial trade and dementation I find these arrangements over generous. Then too I remember Nero Claudius Cæsar and what a hash that young literary artist made of this world when he attempted to control it: and I decide that by and large the cohorts of Æsred manage matters, if not perfectly, at any rate with comparative competence.

27

Embraces a Planet

I PAUSE here to fit a cigarette into one of the paper holders I affect, and finding after a moment's search some matches on the window sill just behind me, I chance to observe upon the half open match box the words "Made in Finland for the So-and-So Company, Pittsburgh, Pa." I note in what a strange and momentous and indeed august performance I am about to take part, now that I round off a world-embracing enterprise and prepare to consummate a more notable triumph than ever filled the Via Sacra with shouts and purple and bay wreaths, with white bulls restively heaving and contorting their gilded horns, and with ungracious captives who trudged chained through the aroused dust without thinking to applaud the splendor with which they too were being escorted toward

166

death. I weigh (to put it more briefly) those same nine words on this box of matches.

Finland seems a remote place. It is a place about which I know nothing. Vague notions of Hans Christian Andersen (who, to be sure, was a Dane) and of Henrik Ibsen (who, now I think of it, was a Norwegian) seem the utmost the word Finland evokes, against a general background of Vikings and fir-trees. Perhaps this two-inch splinter of wood tipped with a dark daub of some dozen chemicals was once part of a fir-tree. It savors to a tentative nibble rather like pine-wood. In any case the tree grew in Finland, where the sun and the rain and the planet under me co-operated to produce the wood splinter which in due course the Finnish cohorts of Æsred made into the especial match I am now twiddling between my thumb and my forefinger, when they blended, to pleasure me, this small brown blob of gum and ground glass and phosphorus and chlorate of potash and I forget just what other matters, well to the other side of the world.

A ship manned by yet other hundreds of them that serve Æsred has brought this match adown the Baltic Sea and through the so engagingly named Kattegat and Skagerrack, and then across the Atlantic. Customs have been paid upon my match before its entry into this country—some while after many congressmen and senators have been at long pains to arrange for me the manner and the cost price of this entry, and after a President also has duly approved (or perhaps he unavailingly vetoed) this part of the work involved in getting my match to me. In both legislative and executive branches the Federal Government has thus toiled for my cosseting. Then (once, of course, the needed preliminaries had been seen to, in the way of building a railroad and of hiring the swart engineers and firemen and brakesmen) a clangorous and reverberative freight train snortingly bore off my match to Pittsburgh, Pa.: and there, in anticipation of my match's arrival, the So-and-So Company had already builded a warehouse or two to contain this match until I needed it.

So much seems clear enough, though even after that my match must be escorted to Richmond in due estate, with yet more brakesmen talkatively carrying lanterns into the night so that they might perform their ritualistic hammering upon the wheels of the freight car in which my match was travelling, and with a peering anchorite on guard in the caboose (with that narrow-eyed pessimism which has marked the tanned face of every caboose man I have ever noted), and looking out for the safety of my match, at each instant during the day time. Or perhaps this box of matches journeyed less tolerantly, in one of those rude blustering vans which pre-empt the highway and oust other traffic into the ditch, in the while that my match came from Pittsburgh, Pa., to the corner grocery store a block behind me,—whence the butler fetched it last week, after the slave trade had imported his ancestors from Africa, and so had produced this final chapter in the great saga of this world-embracing enterprise.

It is bewildering, in fine, to reflect upon the

169

multitudinous machinery and the thousands of my fellow beings that have co-operated so very variously under the guidance of Æsred, in order to enable me to light my cigarette. More people have worked to get this match to me than took part in the siege of Troy, or were involved in the Crucifixion. All this is attested by the words "Made in Finland for the So-and-So Company, Pittsburgh, Pa." And all this has been brought about by Æsred facilely, as a most minor part of the day's work.

Æsred sees to it, I reflect, that at every hour of the day and night I am well served. Not only my matches are brought to me with such pomp and carefulness through the white magics of gregarious compromise. Everywhere in the known world at every instant men are at toil to supply me with food and clothing, to equip my home, to provide me with knickknacks, and to give me something to read about in to-morrow morning's paper.

I look about the little black and silver room, and a glance shows that a planet is my tributary.

If Æsred came to me out of Greece by way of
the Golden House, yet did my cigarette holder
originate in Austria so that it might embrace
tobacco raised in Turkey. That black and silver
tray was made for me in Japan, the silver
stampbox was chased in Holland, and that silver
colored shell was fetched from the bottom of
the Caribbean Sea. Upon the bookcase I observe a black dragon-shaped candlestick from
China standing, between a small black elephant
from Ceylon and a black boar molded in Germany, immediately below the original black
and white drawing for the suppressed cover design for *The High Place* just as Mr. Papé drew
it at Tunbridge Wells. Upon the black mantel
piece (which was quarried in Italy) two small
white china dogs from Czecho-Slovakia are regarding a china polar bear sent to me from
Toronto; and above them I find that steel en-
graving of *The Garden of Love* which Nicolas
de Bruyn completed for me in France in 1604.
I cast down my eyes: the rug underneath me is
from Persia, the rubber heels of my shoes came

from the Dutch East Indies, and I reflect that my socks were woven in Scotland.

It becomes mildly disturbing to observe how very, very many servants Æsred has mustered up to attend me, all over the world, and to note how multifariously they perform for my comfort's sake such extravagant thaumaturgies as no wizard ever wrung from his familiars. In this box of matches, the thought occurs to me, my far-flung lackeys have confined, under Æsred's guidance, the divine power of fire, to the sole end that I may now light my cigarette.

28

A Pantheon in Fir-Wood

WE HAVE all come, of course, to regard a penny box of matches as equally an affair of course. Here, I reflect, here with a vengeance, is an example of the downfall of those gods whom I but now had in mind. And I decide that in a world so very full of the flabbergasting and of the comic, one should not yield to the dullness of regarding anything whatever as a matter of course.

For it seems to me (upon reflection) not wholly an affair of commonplace that in this trumpery box I should carry about, as my prisoner, the inexplicable god to whom was addressed the earliest of all known hymns, when mankind praised "the most high and admirable and excellent Agni, whose power is luminous and very fearful and not to be trusted." They

reported of him, with odd prescience, that this
Agni had been engendered by a coupling of
small sticks much like these match stems, which
had miraculously begotten between them a
shining monster, with seven arms and three legs
and two faces, the one favorable and the other
malignant. They reported that in this guise
Agni went about earth and heaven and mid-air
at his own will, riding sometimes upon a ram,
but at other times in a brazen chariot drawn by
scarlet horses, without ever giving any warning
whether his mood would be kindly or fatal; and
that he was the sole mediator between mankind
and the other gods, to whom he carried the
burnt offerings and the ingratiating incense, for
Agni alone of the Heavenly Ones abode habitually among mankind as an immortal reborn
every day upon the hearthstones of human
homes. They reported that he was a giver of
good things, the purveyor of food and warmth,
the untiring opponent of darkness. But they
reported likewise that he would now and then
(always without the least forewarning) become

174

a destroyer whom even the gods feared, for it was well known how dreadfully Agni had frightened all the other immortals when the Fire God, in order to repair his twitching gait and the yellow biliousness brought on by devouring too many oblations of clarified butter, had eaten the sacred Khandava forest—trees, saplings and bushes in one gulping—as a digestant.

These things and many other things men reported about Agni: he had his temples and his priests, his ritual and his devotees, and his high station in the most old of Trinities, a long while before Jehovah was heard of: and I find it a strange outcome that any god so strong and venerable should lie here trapped at the end of a tiny fir chip.

But if that were all! That is merely the beginning of Æsred's triumph, wherein Agni is but the most elderly of the attendant captives. Here in this box is imprisoned also, I reflect, that ruddy cripple whom the Greeks reported to have been born without any father, and when still in diapers to have been hurled over the ramparts of heaven, so that he fell through the not inconsiderable length of three days, as I recall the affair; and like an infant meteorite plunged sizzlingly into the Mediterranean, where the kind nereids christened him Hephæstos, rearing him in their coral caves at the bottom of this sea. Thence he ascended into heaven, stubbornly, without any graciousness, at his own good hour, to abide as the one creative artist among the gods. In the while that his fellow Kronidês wantoned in strange beds and destroyed mankind as wantonly as a peevish child might rage among toys, this Hephæstos alone toiled laboriously and created imperishable matters,—building to adorn heaven the bright homes of the Olympians, and shaping that large cup in which the sun was suspended, and forging the thunder bolts also, and tipping each of these bolts with a triform rudder of hail and of cloud and of swift wind,—and in this way making of all heaven a more vividly romantic place, just as upon earth he created the flame-breathing bulls of Colchis, and the gold and silver dogs

176

which guarded the house of Alcinoös, and that glittering brass giant man called Talus, and gave life to each of these his miraculous handicraft. The power of this so quiet seeming Hephæstos (like the power of Agni) was thus beneficent in its normal exercise, and yet remained always very fearful and not to be trusted. This lamed drudge lived, in his own chosen way, with such independence that he alone of the immortals had dared to oppose almighty Zeus, in defence of his loved mother Hera, valiantly. In all his doings he was so unpredictable —on account of, the learned said, those subtile poisons which permeate every artist's temperament—that although the Fire God was eternally wedded to beauty, having Aphrodite's fair foam-and-rose colored self for wife, yet he had lusted after wisdom also, even in the icy presence of Pallas Athene, and had assaulted the sublime virgin whom the other gods, as more easy-going divine fribbles, revered and avoided too on account of her sombre and bleak strength.

I might in this place, with an entire diction-

ary to my left hand, continue to build up yet
other noble sentences in memoriam to yet other
Fire Gods were it not that epitaphs are rather
depressing playthings. I remark with Nordic
baldness that here in this box is imprisoned also
that nimble son of the lightning and of the fir-
tree of whom it was reported, boreally, that no
living being knew with any sureness whether
this Loki were the friend or the enemy. He con-
sorted of his own accord with mankind, whom
he aided, always with a certain elvish unrelia-
bility; and through more than one divine crisis
his cunning had preserved even the All-Father
Woden, with yet others of the benign Æsir, in
their celestial headquarters. But Loki's children
were the deformed huge Fenris wolf and Jör-
mungander, the supreme serpent of Midgard,
and Death was the third child of Loki, a child
whom he nurtured lovingly; and it was rumored
that at the coming of the dim day named
Ragnarök this Loki and his three omnivorous
children would destroy all mankind and the benign gods likewise, and that the fertile, wave-

washed earth and all-glorious Valhalla too would then perish, through the power of Loki, that power which was very fearful and not to be trusted.

To-day the power of Loki is imprisoned here, at the tip of a tiny wood sliver. The might of Ahriman, and of Moloch, and of all the Maruts, has been trapped here by the same sorcery: and in this little box is confined likewise the power of Zagnugael, who appeared to the keeper of the flocks of Jethro, upon Mount Horeb, and thus set afoot the liberation of the children of Israel, for which the credit fell by-and-by to another immortal. And many other gods and many potent devils are imprisoned here,—one deity at least for every match in the box,—because in every land and time men have dreaded and have endeavored to placate fire, under one name or another name, on account of their dependence upon the bright friend who gave food and warmth, and on account of their helplessness before the quick-smiting enemy who was luminous and very fearful and not to be trusted.

Well, and in my hand this strange great pantheon lies quiescent. To each one of these fallen deities has been accorded, once, somewhat more of honor and of sincere faith than Jehovah receives under our present scheme of civilization. Each one of the Fire Gods has had his temples, his Holy of Holies, his Bible, his Heaven, and his retinue of angels and bishops and sextons: and of all these belongings Æsred has stripped each one of them lightly. She has made of these incandescent immortals her artisans, her house servants, and her day laborers. Loki has postponed Ragnarök at her bidding and has taken over the duties of a furnace man; Hephæstos humbly attends to her railways and to the transportation facilities in general of the sleek cohorts of Æsred; Agni is at work in her manufacturing plants; and Moloch, that most dreadful one, the child-devourer, who fed insatiably when loud drums sounded in the dark valley of Tophet, waits here in attendance, like a perfectly trained under-butler, ready to light my cigarette.

29
Ends with Apostasy

YES, I reflect, that which I now do commemorates an august victory; and I endeavor to kindle my match with a stroke of some appropriate stateliness. The plump brown head of it crumbles and mashes, and half of it falls away from the match stem. I recollect the brief rainstorm which during the forenoon has wetted this box of matches as it lay by the open window: and I perceive that the might of Æsred has labored, for at least this once, fruitlessly. She has dethroned gods and bridled the force of earth and laid a harness upon the ocean, in order that this small box might travel across the world to me: so that these matches might aid to light my cigarettes she has put, I repeat, a long servitude upon more of my fellow beings than took part in the siege of Troy or were involved in the Crucifixion: and the upshot of all this toil and hazard and marvel working is that the matches, now I have them at last, are of no conceivable use to anybody.

It really does seem an apologue to which one might fit any number of morals. But I educe none of them. I have squandered a deal too much thought upon serious matters, I decide, and it is time an industrious author should get back to his nonsense.

Yet I first look toward the bust of Æsred, not over the top of my reading glasses but through them; and I can thus see her, very far out of focus, only as a vague form which appears pale and implacable and wholly lovely. I imagine that this woman is not Æsred who allures us into the gregarious, kindly rule of conformity. I think that the woman whom I faintly see is that Lady Beauty whom Rossetti also glimpsed with myopic eyes and then hymned as a goddess who compels, "by sea or sky or woman, to one law her allotted bondman,"—and whom yet other poets have seen just thus remotely at one time or another time, and whom thereafter they have served perforce (as men honored the equivocal Lords of Fire) under many names. Keats rhymed of her as La Belle Dame Sans Merci; as Lilith she was necessarily deleted by Moses from a romance meant for family reading; and to Thomas of Ercildoune she came as the Queen of Faëry. But in her name alone is she variable. As Tannhäuser found her in the Hörselberg, and as Homer found her at doomed Troy, even so, without any gray declension or any smirching by common-sense, does the Witch-Woman endure to-day, and she yet haunts the lonely thinking of every true poet with an unabated compulsion.

In the Poictesme which begot Æsred, she was called Ettarre; and men said of Ettarre that her arts were otherwise than are the comfortable arts of Æsred. Ettarre, they avowed, does not incite us to comfort; she cannot give us a box of matches: but she bestows an ecstasy of such sort as (let it once transgress from the tinselled cloister of art into affairs of more solid worth) wise Æsred views with morose indignation. Nevertheless, without heeding Æsred, does Ettarre evoke an outmoded ecstasy. Ettarre remains, in spite of all that Æsred may do to withhold mankind from the dangers of thought and of too high endeavor, Ettarre yet remains the immortal Witch-Woman who calls to the young in heart, half-idly, with an unimaginable sweetness, such as compels her allotted bondman to depart from the asphalt ways of conformity even nowadays, and to go as an outcast into Antan or whithersoever else she may direct, so dear is her favor.

So very dear is her favor, I reflect, that it drew Alfgar to his death in the Garden Between Dawn and Sunrise; it betrayed Black Odo even at the pearly gate of Heaven; it left Madoc a moonstruck vagabond; it has imprisoned me in a small black and silver room between a typewriter and an unabridged dictionary; and of the lives of yet other persons it has made a foiled and forever lonely adventuring sustained with a high heart. For Ettarre teaches that the ways

184

of conformity are wise but ignoble; that the respect of the dullwitted and of the cowed is an
honor somewhat incriminating; and that her
secret knowledge, if only we could master it,
may yet lead some of us, among dim byways,
toward that unique land in which one may live,
perhaps, with more competence. Even in the
ambiguity of that half-promise she lies, no
doubt; but she remains wholly lovely. She is
the lady in domnei of all true romantics,
whether they be young or old.

I find it therefore a considerable comfort that
my reading glasses should require but an instant
to convert Æsred into Ettarre; and it is before
the unreal vision begotten by the frailty of my
failing eyes, and not before any adroitly carven
stone, that I now bend in the attitude of a postu-
lant. I then insert yet another sheet of paper
into my typewriter; I feel the enkindling of a
creative writer's complete if baseless contentment; and I begin upon a new paragraph of that
especial sort of nonsense which happens to divert me more affably than does Æsred's wisdom.

*ON A JOURNEY
IN WINTER*

Tread softly and circumspectly in this funambulatory track. Consider whereabout thou art in Cebes's table, or that old philosophical pinax of the life of man: whether thou art yet in the road of uncertainties; whether thou hast yet entered the narrow gate, got up the hill and asperous way, which leadeth unto the house of sanity; or taken that purifying potion from the hand of sincere erudition, which may render thee clean and pure.

30

*Toys and *Analogues*

HE wind is, to the
painstaking ear, just
audible now that after
a happy day's playing
before Æsred, I settle
down in the well-
padded, large green chair near the glowing
fireplace. Night has fallen sullenly: for Decem-
ber rules outside, held in check by the fragile
thickness of a window pane: and about the wide,
cold and livid street (which the arc-lights at the
corner have now made so like the corpse of a
street) this wind blunders as an agreeably restless reverberancy rather than as an absolute
noise. I approve of this sedative and in some sort
flattering wind. This vagabond wind is at labor,
in its humble way, to emphasize the warm snug-

ness of my shelter and the discreetly lighted, quiet order about me.

To the unsympathetic, no doubt, a great deal within eyeshot would savor less strongly of order than of the oriental bazaar and of the antique shop, yet I regard my toys with approval. Upon the glass-topped mahogany table near the room's centre my metal playthings catch and reflect the firelight's moving quite handsomely, I consider, where the small bright rabbit and the camel and the lion and the lizard and the turtle and the giraffe and yet other miscellaneous brass fauna, some sixteen in number, are ranged about the comparatively large brass stallion. My china playthings confront me upon the crowded mantel piece, where a white stallion rears at either side of the clock among twenty-five smaller animals: and they confront me also upon the thronged tops of the low book shelves at either side of the room, in a gaily colored dwarfed mob of most of the beasts and birds and reptiles familiar to natural history, with a liberal admixture of creatures not as yet classified by scientists. Nor is this quite all, for above them, upon the high half-window ledges, perch two green Foo-dogs and a yet larger white stallion.

I recall that my last census-taking showed a hundred and forty-odd of these various animals; and I wonder at my persistent childishness in collecting such trumpery stuff; but even so, I do regard them contentedly. They are quaint; they are upon their minute scale gaudy; and I may here cherish a frank liking for the rococo, for the embroidered, and for the spangles of stylistic excess, without having to consider (here at least) the more astringent tastes of other persons, inasmuch as this room is my own private playground.

From a complacent survey of the toys set about my library I turn now to regard my attendants. One is, I decide, very well attended hereabouts. It is flattering to observe how many and how widely different persons throng from all castes and eras, in cloth and boards and leather, to offer you diversion. I consider the hundreds who mutely woo me with so much of the best that human wisdom and human imagination have produced; and I attempt to regard my postulants with the restrained gravity befitting my estate,—I who am, in this especial room and thus far at least, their expected messiah. The great and the agreeable are mustered here in dress parade. The most of them have looked forward to this meeting with me for some centuries. Each stands upon my shelves with, as it were, his best foot foremost,—with his weak points concealed, with his talents artfully burnished, and with his every utterance pumped up to that false magnanimity which custom demands of a self-respecting writer,—and each tacitly solicits my favor now that I come among them as posterity.

A library, I reflect, is a topsy-turvily companionable place wherein we are enfranchised to consort with, and may even deliciously patronize, our superiors. Under its club privileges the most sluggish in spirit may presume to dismiss Cæsar as the primal liar among all war correspondents, or to deride Cyrano to his deformed face (in the form of a frontispiece), or to jeer at the great Frederick's French verse-making, with a frankness which common prudence denied to these quick warmen's flesh-and-blood contemporaries. A library is a republic, an economically neutral republic lying between the belligerent kingdoms of good and evil; and it entertains large embassies from both neighbors amicably. A library is time's lockbox, reserved for time's chief treasures; a library is a zoölogical garden wherein thoughts which were once wild now live without zest in their neatly ticketed cages; and a library is also a pathological exhibit of dreams very badly damaged during the throes of birth.

Yet other analogues occur to me. But above all a library is a retreat in which no fret nor any trouble may long endure; if we preserve low thoughts in its sanctuary, there is no excuse. So inflammable indeed is the nature of a ready reader that, for my part, I find two minutes' labor in the proper pages will suffice handsomely to inflate me with religious awe, or with patriotism, or with the most broad-minded sort of philanthropy; nor is there any other benefi-cent virtue which a library will not lend to its frequenters gratis. It is a weak frisk of sophism to say (as my doubts say now) that these emo-tions are not lasting. You would not (I severely remind myself in rebuttal), no, not even you, I hope, would consider scorning your dinner on the ground of its impermanency; and very much as this ever-transient round of dinners sustains the human body, so may the uncostly and short-lived emotions that are begotten by fine litera-ture be esteemed to keep strong and nimble man's mind.

—To which my doubts reply, But look at your mind after all these many years of reading! And I punish, naturally, their display of any such rudeness by dismissing these doubts.

31
Considers a Dark Magic

EVEN SO, I reflect, this library is a catacomb in which each book is a tomb; and I who disturb its quietness visit the grim place like an improvident necromancer. I revive, as the whim takes me, one or another of the dead, where but for my unwholesome arts would decay peacefully each uncharmed compost of rags and glue and oak gall and macerated wood splinters. I offer an initiatory strange sacrifice, of time and of eyesight: thereafter it is at my sheer election whether Thackeray buttonholes me with mildly shabby Victorian scandals, or majestic Virgil arises austere and laurel-crowned amid a mock warfare of over-perfectly drilled hexameters, *quadrupedante sonitu*, or the great Ouida returns from out of her more dusty Elysium attended by the élite in basques and crinoline or in curly side-whiskers and rather remarkably baggy trousers.

That which the dead saw once I am then privileged to see very much as when upon clear evenings I observe the light which shone upon Altair or Sirius ever so many thousands of years before we arose from the supper table. The dark magic that men name reading enables whosoever will to pass with long ago entombed companions about Troy or Iceland or Calvary, and to share in the local gossip. Now the somewhat sophomoric daring of dead Marlowe, and now the light and childlike sensuousness of dead Swinburne, is kindled transiently in the reader's more prosaic brain cells; for all our faculties are enlarged and obsessed in this necromantic yielding so that our normal senses are not any longer controlled undividedly.

To the contrary, one may appraise superterrestrial matters with Dante's pious and diamond-hard eyes quite as facilely as one may sniff at all such unphilosophical nonsense with Gibbon's little pug nose: and one does. Temporarily your lips are visited by the faint and gravely wistful smile of Montaigne: it fades now that you are tranced by a music more old than Rome, which Homer is hearing yet again through the aid of your personal ears, or perhaps your eyelids twitch with the same local throbbing which forewarned Theocritus that Amaryllis was about to come forth from her shadowy cavern among the pale fern fronds and swaying ivy leaves. For a while the broad lustiness of great Gloriana's time is at riot in a reader's genital organs, and all plackets bid him stand and deliver: at another season he is wooing more seriously, and even with some element of hopefulness, a woman who but barely predeceased his grandparents.

We are illuded thus handsomely, and very dreadfully, in the while that our lungs move with long perished laughter, and our eyes brim with the tears of the dead. It is far wide of the mark to declare (as Oscar Wilde has declared, in his dealing with this same necromancy) that at such times "dead lips have their message for us, and hearts which have fallen into dust can communicate their joy." The affair strikes more deep: for the dead then possess us. It is their aspirations and their loves and their desires which animate us rather than the emotions proper to our own experience. We believe for the moment that which we know to be untrue, and value beyond Samarkand and Ophir creeds in which we have no least faith. We give over, in brief, our nerves and our minds and our judgments to the dead; and our natures are violated by the ghosts we have evoked through the dark magic of reading.

I dismiss these uncomfortably necrophilic reflections, which have beguiled me into what I prefer to regard as nonsense expressed in an over labored prose passage. I look again at my china toys. I observe beneath them the arrayed books which are many-colored and gaily gilded traps set for me. I perceive that the dead authors of these books now lurk about me like vampires forever ready to be requickened into a half-hour or so of transient life in the flesh and blood of posterity: and I discomfit all their grisly artfulness by electing for that old tale about Prince Asuga which an unknown barbarian made very long ago in his Himalayan uplands without any thought of posterity.

32

The Essential Outline

As I READ in comfort, I observe that the wind
continues to speak inaudibly of dissatisfactory
matters. It goes about my snug home aimlessly.
There is in this wind no vehemence. It grum-
bles, but it seems to grumble without large conviction. It displays at utmost the formal fretful-
ness of a woman who has for the moment no
particular fault to find with her husband, or
perhaps it murmurs with the aggrieved re-
pressedness of a poor relation.

Indeed, as I recall my Dickens, it is a sort of
Twemlow among winds,—constrained and small
and inefficient and monotonous, without any
claim upon human consideration beyond its
cousinship to an aërial peerage. One cannot out
of hand believe that this depressed wind comes
of the high-spirited race of hurricanes such as

so mightily deject the stock market when they visit Florida and of the cloudbursts which every once in a while sweep hitherto inconspicuous Western villages into the news reels of gilded moving picture palaces. It reaches me only as a vague noise, now rising slightly and now sinking toward stillness, but not ever ceasing utterly. There is no animosity in this wind, I assure myself; and it lulls me as I turn again, in yet undisturbed contentment, to Southern Asia.

I am reading, be it repeated, the old tale of Prince Asuga. I read of his divinely appointed journey in quest of the five kettledrums,—and of how he inadvertently ate the shah's peacock, and of how he fought with Sakra (when that lustful demon wore the form of a crowned worm with copper-colored eyes), and of how he practised the sixty-four arts of love with the accomplished daughter of a Kadali tree, and of how he surprised the Princess Manohara in her cedar-walled bathing chamber with nine large astonishments, and of how Prince Asuga performed yet many other fine exploits, during the

course of his gay journeying from South Pan-
chala to the Emerald Palace at Naireb.

Then as I look up toward my small collection
of volumes dealing with myth and magic, to the
right of the fireplace, I comprehend that the
essential outline of this tale is retraced there in
thousands upon thousands of variants: and I
put aside the book to reflect that in all folklore
the human hero must leave that which is familiar, to journey upon a quest. Throughout
those eight tall shelves it is the hall mark of
every mortal champion that he should leave his
wonted home and the faces which are known,
to go in search of what is remote and strange to
him,—whether the brisk youngster aspire to win
a golden-haired princess or to despatch an op-
pressive monster or to fetch back one of those
conveniently portable magic articles such as
romance clung to childishly throughout its
infancy.

On the journey the adventurer rests, if but
overnight, at this or the other strange place,
where he meets with improbable happenings.

He is beset by outlaws or trolls or afrits, he has perilous dealings with vampires or with warlocks, and sorceresses or swan maidens may also attempt to beguile him; but he escapes from every ill-wisher through the friendly offices of an ant or of an eagle whose life he has saved, or it may be through the aid of a talisman he happens to have found a bit earlier. Undamaged, he journeys on to yet another place, traversing a highway which the champion has never trod before, and which he is not ever again to revisit: but here too he deals thrivingly with the customs of the local giants and magic-mongers and with that strange foible of the more ancient royal families for asking riddles.

He survives every testing, for the young man is resourceful as well as brave. So he manages to heal the afflicted emperor of his illness, whether with a golden apple or with the ashes of a blue flower or with some yet other standard prescription from the pharmacopœia of romance; he makes off, still unhurt, with the ogre's loquacious harp; he gallops intrepidly up the side of the glass mountain which none other could scale; and he everywhere leaves behind him a red wake of slain tyrants and dragons. Thus handsomely do affairs speed from one outlandish realm to another, until in the courteous old unveracious way of thorough-going romanticists the tale-teller rounds off all by permitting the resistless and gay adventurer's quest, whatsoever it may happen to embrace, to become wholly successful.

Then the tall lad returns home, whether with a fond princess riding behind him on his saddle or with the wood demon's head swung there gorily adrip; or perhaps he fetches back in his knapsack the Soldan's oily black beard, or the blue goose that lays golden eggs, or the three singing hazel leaves, or the water of life, or whatsoever other knickknack was the goal of his questing. The point is that in any case he has done with the rough and tumble of foreign travel. Amid the acclaim of his neighbors he settles down to domestic life; the king regnant in that locality dies with a most friendly promp-

204

titude; the young hero is chosen as a matter of course to be ruler over the whole realm; he governs it with valor and prosperity, and he lives (we are told in the folklore of primitive nations) happily ever afterward.

33

De Omnibus

WHEN a quest is finished, then its achiever lives
happily ever afterward. Such at least, I reflect as
I sit at my fireside, was the bland ending of the
first fireside tales designed solely to divert a
youthful-spirited and uncritical audience. But
soon and very soon the strong destroyer which
is called common-sense stalked brusquely into
folklore, proclaiming that in point of fact no
human story could ever end thus: and the tale-
tellers yielded to this wholly unæsthetic form of
criticism, by admitting that the heroic also may
attain to middle life and to the one or the other
of its romantically inadmissible sequels. Nor
was this surrender made lately. Such "realism"
began in the remote infancy of tale-telling,
when the Greeks displayed upon this point also
their customary ignorance of classical standards.

De Omnibus

The Greek heroes, as we all know, went upon quests in their youth's heyday, and they succeeded in these quests after the time-honored routine: but furtive little legends which mankind never took to heart and most resolutely did not cherish in memory—these whispered uncheerfully, in a sordid and quite modern vein of "realism," as to what happened afterward to Odysseus, and Heracles, and Theseus, and Jason, and to all the other of these high-hearted adventurers, telling how each one of them came to exile and to poverty and to senile lusts and at last to death in some ironically casual form. I regard the two squat volumes upon the top shelf wherein Apollodorus has garnered his sad examples of the very latest school of biography. I remember that aged Jason was killed by the falling of a tree, and that the last exploit of gray Theseus was to tumble over a cliff; I recall that both Heracles and Odysseus were accidentally poisoned in late middle life—the one with a second-hand shirt and the other with the scratch of a fishbone. Through such bitter contrivances,

and as if with a derisory snarl, did the old tale-
tellers come, in the faraway babyhood of fiction,
to emphasize man's human dislike of the fixed
ending for all human daring and vigor, howsoever heroically these may have been exercised
in the brief season of their prime.

The gods who in the various old tales (up
yonder to the right of my fireplace) either
abetted or opposed the human adventurer differed remarkably. These gods were as widely
various as are my china toys, I reflect, for man
has shaped his gods in accordance with his secret
humility; and myth-makers have agreed only
that these overlords upon whom depended all
mortal destinies were so gratifyingly unlike human beings as to be quite competent to handle
human affairs. It would appear that man, view-
ing ruefully his own weakness, has observed
with even more of awe than of envy all visible
forms of superhuman vigor; and so at one time
or another has respectfully endowed his gods
with the fervor of the sun and the genital reliability of the bull and the cold serpent's

fearlessness. At yet other seasons of devout meditation he has allied his divine care-takers with such disparate kindred as are clouds and alcohol and oak-trees and oceans and thunderbolts and sprouting corn, in the while that his troubled senses noted the incomprehensible vigor which informed each one of these unexplained phenomena; and assumed as a matter of course, rather than of strict logic, that all vigor was somehow consecrated to the furthering of mankind's welfare, alike upon earth and in heaven.

Even I, the wind reminds me diffidently, have been among men's gods. I was Eolus, holding a perpetual revel behind those high walls of brass which made inaccessible my drifting island. I was Jahveh, abluster in the lightnings of Sinai. I was the All-Father Woden, that Eternal Huntsman, exceedingly well mounted upon an eight-legged mare and attended by ravens. I was Tezcatlipoca also, wandering over all the earth to stir up strife and war. And I have borne many other names.

Putting aside the divine claims of my visitant, I remark only that the gods differed; and the old tales about them differed. But every one of the old tales wherein a human being figures as the protagonist is of a piece in its main outline. The man goes upon a journey: that is all. It may be that, as in the stories of Bellerophon or of Raymondin de la Forêt or of the Princes Amgiad and Assad, he journeys in flight from a threatened danger. It may be that as the little tailor or as the self-ennobled Marquis of Carabas he journeys in patched breeches and complete impudence with merely a large notion of making his fortune. It may be that, as Lancelot or Gawaine, he journeys from the portcullis of Camelot, very superb in shining steel and dyed leather and fluent with gay silks and fringes, as a sort of special constable to enforce everywhere the chivalrous virtues; as Kilhwch he may journey over-lightly into a demon-haunted forest as he follows after strange brindled grayhounds that have strong collars of rubies about their necks; or perhaps in the rude hauberk and the

winged helmet of Siegfried the human hero journeys toward Isenland merely to see marvels and to seek out high adventures.

The inciting motives are thus various: but by ordinary a quest is involved, since the most obvious inducement for going upon a journey is that you have some especial business to discharge at your destination. The point is, the legend weavers saw to it that in any event, and through whatsoever causes, the human hero did go upon a journey; and his history in every branch of folklore became the record of what happened to him in that journey through unfamiliar places whose highways he had never trodden before and was not ever again to revisit.

So was it, I reflect, and so was it alone, that the old tale-tellers who concocted all those volumes to the right of my fireplace would appear to have seen human life—as a man journeying. So was it that all religions have seen human life, as a man journeying through this world toward the bright rewards or the bale fires of another world. So did the great shaper of parables discourse of the journeys which were made by the lord of the vineyard and by the prodigal son into a far country, and by a certain traveller toward Jericho, and by the good shepherd into the wilderness. So for that matter do the scientists (at present) assure us that human life is but a stage in the long journey of evolution; and just so, in the lately departed days when people rode upon railway trains, did the stories told in all smoking compartments deal with the adventures of a travelling salesman.

That formula alone is current in every branch of fiction: there was once such and such a man; and through this or the other reason he was forced to go upon a journey; and in his journeying so and so happened to him. That is the archetype of fables: and I imagine it is about this same fable that the wind has been speaking inaudibly from the very first.

34
Dwells Airily Upon Truisms

THIS wind assures me, somehow, that I, too, have retold the old fable, over and yet over again, without ever really understanding it. Here, though, I would distinguish. In my dealings with the folklore of Poictesme I have often wondered at the inhabitants' fixed predisposition (with which I have not any sympathy whatever) to go upon a quest and a journey. All through the Biography of the life of Manuel I have noted (with not infrequent perturbation) how quite strangely ready was every one of that life's embodiments to drop the ties of his legal home and to be off upon this or the other journey. It was to no purpose that I disapproved as a sober householder; as a sober historian I could but record the unquestioned facts.

Yonder are the resultant eighteen volumes,

where my paper playthings stand in fit order beneath my china playthings. Yonder is Manuel upon a journey, and Madoc, and Guivric, and Coth, and Jurgen, and Florian, and Gerald, and all the countless others who went upon one or another journey among matters and happenings but very inadequately explained to them. They went upon this journey among ever-present mysteries, the wind tells me, not altogether for the reasons which you imagined in the while you played their historian. They went upon this journey because that is the one universal story and the one fate which stays decreed for every person.

—Even though (says the wind, with a mild hoot), even though he may superficially appear to sit snug at home and tamely to await burial in the same parish wherein he was christened. It is permitted no man not to leave his wonted home and the faces which are known. Your Horace had the truth of it: you are all bound on one journey, which you begin in diapers and finish in a shroud. You journey from the cradle to the schoolroom and so to the puzzled ardors and the blundering desires of your prime. You journey thence toward the more sedative workaday life of offices and counting houses and courts of law and quiet libraries; you journey toward the farther side of official desks and of typewriters and of shop counters: so do you journey perforce from out of your youthfulness toward one or another means of earning that daily food which will sustain you to continue journeying. You journey toward marriage and parenthood, goaded after the manner of beasts by the blind and irresistible instincts of a beast. You journey toward fattening wits and more sluggish senses and the stigma of public approval, now that you journey as a well-thought-of citizen. Though the vigor and the desire die out of you like guttering candles, do you oldsters yet pluck up heart, and know that you still journey quite as speedily as may the alert young, in the while that you all journey together toward a black door with silver-plated handles. And at no moment of your journey is there any pausing as you travel upon that part of a highway which you have never trodden before and are not ever again to revisit.

You may not manage (the wind here remarks, with yet another apt literary allusion), you may not manage, as the Red Queen alone has managed by running her utmost, to stay where you are. At each instant you go forward, will-you or nill-you, upon a journey wherein all human ties and friendships cool and fall away. Enmities cool also, and dwindle in the dim huddle of dead years behind you; each woman that was dearest is recalled by-and-by as but a sort of emotional mile post in your journeying: for you may neither love nor hate with a graying heart; and the exalted emotions of his youth remain far, oh, very far, behind every reputable way-farer, as half forgotten uplands through which the traveller passed once, and which he may not hope to revisit. Each journeys steadily beyond the desires and the ways of thinking which at any present moment were his. There is no passion which endures, no desire which stays fervent, and no comrade who remains near to the eternal journeyer. He may not hope to touch permanence anywhere. Not even in his own being may he look to find permanence, for that being alters unceasingly, alike in its physical body and in spirit and in needs and in intelligence. As the shape of a cloud is altered in its drifting, so do your virtues and your beliefs take momentary form and then melt away acquiescently into some other shaping in the while that you journey; and so must all men change at every instant in their noisy journey through a continuous changing until the supreme change has created its quiet carrion.

You too (the wind observes, with an uncivil lapse into rather more directly personal criticism) have journeyed a long way; and you have come safely, somehow—through how many veering tides of chance, among time's steady ruining, among what odd wrecks of effort and of aspiration and of compromise!—to the ease of this quiet room. It would be pleasant to remain here in this tranquillity which you have earned and

have paid for very variously, with a great deal
of work and of double-dealing and of self-denial
and of irrational obstinacy. You rest here, at
ease, among your flimsy toys. To the right hand
and to the left gleam the bright and frail symbols of your life's rewards. It would be pleasant
to retain your wonted home and the faces which
are known. Now that the long quest of the Biography is done with, it would be wholly pleasant
to have done with all further journeying also,
after the complete fashion of a fireside tale, and
to retain, in default of some higher lot, your
smug form and substance and your contentment
here.

Then the wind says: Now I, who have not any
substance and no form, I who have found no
contentment, I go about your home without any
wrathfulness. I shake tentatively at a window
frame, and I loosen a spray or so of ivy from
your walls. That is all, for to-night. To-night I
reconnoitre here, and I do nothing more in this
place to-night. But I am that unresting wind
which hovers about each home that man has

ever built to be the harbor of his contentment and about every monument which he has raised to commemorate his exceeding mightiness. I am that wind which Heraclitus heard; and I taught him that all flows as I, and I only, decree, but into what deep haven I have not taught Heraclitus nor any other man. I am that wind which Villon heard in the while that he rhymed shiveringly of how I had swept away the emperors and the dauphins and the aureoled martyrs and the bright blaring heralds and the spruce page boys too, all pell-mell, all lost in a dim incoherency everywhere aglitter with their scattered tinsels. I am that wind which Queen Morvyth heard impatiently in the pride of her youth when I went about the Isles of Wonder and whispered that the most lovely of queens may come by-and-by to be lank bones and little maggots. So do I speak with every person at one time or another time when the man sits alone among his frail toys, and when I remind him there is but one fable which holds true everywhere. The man goes upon a journey: that is all.

35

Some Obvious Answers

To THE effect which I have recorded does the
wind speak in the while that I listen as civilly as
I can well manage to this naïve strange wind,—
a wind which really does seem a thought out of
place among the asphalt and the electric lights
and the motor cars and the radio poles of a
thriving up-to-date city. I have not, to be sure,
any particular quarrel with the wind's iterancy
of these self-evident truths. In fact the more cal-
low young, in common with every known major
poet, have considered all these highflown axioms with some actual profit in the way of verse-
making. Yet age teaches us the pragmatic value
of ignoring these truths; and this pseudo-lyric
nonsense, which is natural enough, and in a
limited sense even pardonable, to winds come
out of the far Isles of Wonder, has become not

quite the sort of nonsense to be regarded seriously by a responsible householder who lives in a common-sense world.

I rather fancy myself as a responsible householder; and I adorn the rôle with the most realistic touches. Though this ingrained habit of writing books may allure me into some time-wasting now and then, I have painstakingly learned how to divert myself with such practical matters as the condition of my bank balance and of my modest investments in the stock market. Indeed upon several occasions I have almost persuaded myself that I could very nearly understand the incurred statements from the bank and the brokers. Then one has always the month's bills to be considered without any frivolity; and taxes, both State and Federal, help to lend my middle life a becomingly serious cast.

An astute author must constantly keep in progress this or the other wary argument with his publishers; and he lives in a perpetually invigorating feud with the printers and the computations of the auditing department. Apart from these inevitable business affairs, my personal correspondence alone, if I did not neglect it with untiring fidelity, would consume the working hours of each week. To how many thousands, I wonder, have I typed a note about the pronouncing of my surname, or about my inability to autograph this or the other book! And domesticity also files an ever-lively claim upon the attention. The responsible householder, for example, may hardly decide without due debate whether we shall have a roast of some sort or just chicken again for next Sunday's dinner; who among this year's débutantes have to be entertained formally; what magazines to discontinue; how the weather promises; whether to give that new bootlegger a trial order; or what exact sums we can manage to subscribe this year to the Protestant Episcopal Church and to the Community Fund.

In the time that I am not writing, yet further common-sense problems arise, such as our pressing need of new rugs or wine glasses or table linen or something else in the way of house-furnishings. The question whether or not to retain the current butler may be described with cool moderation as amaranthine. Moreover, one but too often has to hear explained the harsh fallacies involved in the very idea—since for some occult reason ideas become far more revolting when they are very—that a self-respecting woman can go out anywhere in that old rag of an evening dress after one's own sister-in-law has just come back from New York with her trunkfuls of finery. That too (as is mentioned) seems a plain matter of common-sense: and to hear these explanations through to their trenchant coda consumes yet more time and money.

Nor here nor even hereabouts has the long tale its ending. Common-sense demands yet other concernments of the responsible householder. This or that, for example, has to be done for the welfare of the five children and—a really staggering thought—of the five grandchildren too, nowadays. Under the same rational dictates food has to be purchased for the goldfish; the barber has to be visited; the front yard

223

hedges also must be kept trimmed; the more caustic notices of one's latest book (now that one is being demolished in the old sturdy style by yet a fourth generation of reviewers) have to be put out of mind; one must confer more frequently with physicians; and the oil-heater and the motor car and the radio set, they likewise need continually to be tinkered with. In addition to these varied matters of plain duty even the most sedate are now and then perturbed by the unsettling influence of sexual desire, when wedding presents have to be bought at an aggrieved compromise between what the receivers will probably expect and what we can possibly afford. Nor will death tactfully avoid the middle-aged until his business becomes urgent: almost every morning an unlooked-for funeral notice in the day's paper raises the question whether we simply have to send flowers or can just drive by and leave our cards at the door.

So does this or the other common-sense matter perpetually require settlement at the expense of my preferred form of hedonism. So

224

does it come about that, except in those profit-less moments when I am writing polished and thrice polished and then repolished prose, with a demented and uncontagious enjoyment, the responsible householder really has not the time to bother about winds blowing out of the far Isles of Wonder.

36

We Rest in Philistia

EVEN though I lack time to waste upon discursive winds, I reflect, yet am I willing to accept this wind's analogue without demur. Though I too am bound upon a not yet ended journey, I find this especial stage of it to be extremely agreeable. I enjoy playing at the responsible householder. I have, for that matter, enjoyed—by and large—the entire fifty-odd years of my journeying. In the main I have done what I most wanted to do; and my life has turned out —upon the whole—in fair consonance with my general plans. As to what might happen beyond this especial stage, the stage at which I could look upon yonder eighteen green volumes as tangible and finished things, I have never tendered to Providence any overweening advice.

I have ventured, though, my incurious

guesses as to those just not impossible 'fifties
which at that time seemed as far away from me
as to-night seem the Isles of Wonder: and I now
recall that especial guess which I recorded, a
diuturnity or two ago, as to what my present
period in life might be like when one actually
did come, at an inconceivably long last, to journey through it. As I imagined the outcome, a
reflective person might then say, in a quiet
blend of humility and wonder:

"I, like every other man of my years, have in
my day known more or less every grief which the
world breeds; and each maddened me in turn,
just as in time, and after no great while, each
one of them was duly salved by time; so that
to-day their ravages vex me no more than do the
bee-stings I got when I was an urchin. To-day I
grant the world to be composed of muck and
sunshine intermingled; but, upon the whole, I
find the sunshine more pleasant to look at, and
—greedily, because my time for sight-seeing is
not very long—I stare at it. And I hold this creed
to be the best of all imaginable creeds,—that if

we do nothing very wrong, all human imbro-
glios, in some irrational and quite incomprehensible fashion, will be straightened to our sat-
isfaction."

It really seems rather strange. Every phrase of
that, in so far as I am concerned, has turned out
to be an excellent guess, even though I cannot
(at first glance) divine my reasons for including
those two "very's" so very close together. The
words written in my youth, out of illimitable ignorance, prove to be wholly true now that I consider them in the light of annually assured
knowledge: and I seem with precision to have
recorded my present unassertive and tranquil
frame of mind some twenty-odd years before its
arrival. To-morrow and the day after to-morrow
will, I am certain, be found much more dis-
agreeable wayfaring; in fact a man of my age
who still retains his teeth, his tonsils and his
appendix cannot regard himself as other than a
bag of potential high explosives: but with this
particular stage in my journey I do not pick any
least fault. I am grateful for having reached it.

228

WE REST IN PHILISTIA

I view with approval the quiet order about me. The month's bills have been duly paid: I have my wife and the five children and the five grandchildren and my eighteen volumes and my hundred and forty-some small china and brass animals. There is a fairly sound roof overhead, and sufficient food in the pantry, and nearly two hundred and fifty gallons of petroleum in the oil-heater, and a bottle of excellent whisky in the cellarette. These things will every one of them be taken away from me by-and-by; meanwhile I do have them: and it is pleasant to have them, if only as transient loans. I return due thanks to Whosoever may be the cause of my having these loans.

Thereafter I shift the light a bit nearer to my book. I dismiss from thought the various persons that I have been in more hot-blooded periods. No one of them would have liked this toy-littered, middle-class room, or would have put up for one instant with the humble-minded and time-battered person who sits in the abating glow of its firelight reading a childish fairy tale.

But I, I am well content to remain here, for my permitted season, as a responsible householder who lives in a common-sense world and endeavors to honor its rulings not too seriously.

I continue my reading with complete contentment. My toys stand thick about me, mine for at least to-night; I desire to have nothing changed; and the nonsense of a lachrymose and pompous wind now lulls me pleasantly enough as it goes wailingly about my temporary lodgings.

EPILOGUE OF
TRUE THOMAS
BY MOONLIGHT

"Now ye maun go wi' me," she said;
"True Thomas, ye maun go wi' me."

The Happy Ending

I T IS known that in the days of his first youth Thomas Learmont encountered, in a place where three roads met, a thin dark girl who rode upon a stallion that gleamed like silver. Her mantle was of green velvet, and her silken gown also displayed the gray-green color of fern leaves: about the neck of the stallion hung fifty and nine small silver bells. She spoke: and Thomas Learmont very ardently kissed her laughing lips into silence.

She said: "That was over brave. Now your lips cannot ever lie to me, True Thomas."

He replied, "My doom is at one with my desire."

They rode together upon the back of the gleaming stallion along a road which was bordered by ferns everywhere, and they forded a sullen river of which the waters were colored like human blood, coming thus into a garden, and in the midst of this garden they found a tree. They rested in its wavering shadows amicably. She who was the Queen of Faëry had smiled upon mortal lovers before this time, but never at any time had her light body nestled within the strong arms of a human lad who had Thomas Learmont's fancifulness in his talking or such earnestness in all his amicable doings.

It is known that after seven years Thomas Learmont returned into the world wherein mortal beings rule and order matters. He brought with him his memories of a kingdom wherein all were young, and the control of many little half-magics, which he embellished with a poet's innate inventiveness and some legerdemain. He prospered as a reliable and sober soothsayer, with a fair grounding in the nine geomancies. He became well-to-do, and he lived

234

at ease in the serene afternoon of his lifetime, now that all the neighbors who took any thought for the future rode toward Ercildoune with one fee or another fee for True Thomas: the earls, the barons and the dukes talked privately with him about what was to befall them: the King of Scots also sent for True Thomas, and it was in this way the high King learned that because of the passing of the fatal stone Lia-Fail from out of his kingdom, his race must perish, and the detested Bruce would beget new rulers over Scotland.

There had been no sense whatever in telling old Sandy that, and to be doing it was exactly like Thomas Learmont, when you knew it would only upset his majesty and be of no earthly good to anybody, said the wife of Thomas Learmont.

Thomas Learmont mildly agreed to all this, and then said mildly, "Nevertheless ——"

"—— With," she continued, "the soothsaying business what it always is at this time of year, and you know that as well as I do!"

Nodding gravely, Thomas Learmont replied that the seer must speak the truth as it is revealed to him. His wife referred to stuff and nonsense in the while she went on patching the breeches of their third son, and, besides that, she added, you make up more than half of it.

"But not all of it, my dear," said Thomas Learmont. "A fair half of my trade is pure magic, and it is that which puzzles me. I am become at times an impostor, in a world wherein that foible is more or less common to every professional man. But at other times my magic is a true magic, and my looking runs very lightly over all the days which are to come before my client has quite done with earth's daylight; and at these times I must tell, will I or will I not, the truth about my foreseeings, because my lips once touched the lips of the Queen of Faëry."

At that his large and light-colored wife looked at him over the top of her spectacles during the chilled instant that she said, reflectively:

"Lips! And the things I have heard about that woman!"

The Happy Ending

Thomas Learmont fidgeted. "Well, but, my dear," he remarked, "a wife always does hear these things, somehow or another. And more often than not, I can give my clients something far more acceptable than the truth about their future. So these passing seizures of veracity do not really injure my soothsaying."

38

As to Several Magics

THE matters thus far recorded are known. To many persons it is not known that in the spring of the year, upon the last night in April, gray Thomas Learmont went by moonlight to a place where three roads met. The one road passed among briers, and lilies grew thickly about the second road, but the third road was bordered by the dim green of many ferns. It was in this place that Thomas Learmont thought about his severance from the thin dark girl and about the noble times when he had thrived as a king in Faëry.

He sighed as he waited there in the moonlight of April. He saw the little white shapes which scuttered and flickered along the briery road, and he saw the little yellow shapes which capered like pale flames in the road that went

238

among lilies, as one by one these shapes fared out of the world wherein mortal beings rule and order matters. In the road which was bordered by ferns the moonlight lay unbroken by anything except the wavering shadows of one tree; not any soul travelled upon this road: and that seemed a large pity to the aging charlatan, now that he remembered the wavering shadows of another tree, and his wisdom was clouded by the betraying magic of April.

This is a magic which has had many analysts, along with its victims, and its effects upon the young in heart have been duly recorded. It is a luxuriant and a very various magic, which, if it flowers now and then with red murder and with long despair and with ill-considered marriages, yet blossoms also with fine poems and with heart-shaking joys. But it blossoms too with a regretting, by-and-by: and a regretting now overshadowed the wisdom and the contentment of Thomas Learmont. A regretting made his snug cottage, and the two acres that he held in fee, and his wife's thrifty housekeeping, and his

239

three sturdy boys, and his two fat cows, and his decent riding horse, and the respect paid to his half-magics by persons who hoped to profit by them, and all the other comforts of a prospering soothsayer, seem to be not quite enough to breed any complacency. All these were plain and solid goods: and the shadow which had come into his thinking made shadows seem more lovely and more dear to him.

So he despatched a little magic of his own shaping, with a lamb's skin, and with mint and marjoram and rosemary, and with three nails from the coffin of a young child. He duly invoked the spirits of Malkuth and the bright lords of Netsah and Hod, to protect and cleanse and enlighten his desire; and the power of this little magic did not fail him. Then Thomas Learmont laughed, now that the Queen of Faëry had returned to him who in the remote days of his youthfulness had been her lover.

240

39

Records the Wrong Words

HE SAID, "The years have been long and without any savor ——" He said then, "Since you went away ——" He cried with a tinge of wildness: "Men have made for me no words to serve my last need! Men have not any words for the passion and the thought which are troubling me!"

She did not answer: but the dark eyes of her eternal youth regarded the old fellow fondly; her young lips smiled with an unforgotten tenderness; and her light young hands lay at this time upon his shrunk and knotted hands, as though the long years of their separation had never been.

Then Thomas Learmont said: "You alone mattered. All that has mattered in my life is that I once had your love. Now that I become old I

do not any longer try to evade this knowledge.
The gray who have only death before them do
not marvel to observe that behind them also
there is only ruin. Yet I marvel, O my dearest,
to hear men acclaiming the deeds performed in
that part of my life which did not matter, and
to see the respectfulness in these dull men's
eyes. I am skilled in this magic or in the other
magic, they report of me, and I have performed
small wonders competently such as no other
man has happened to perform before me. I
think that perhaps this is true: it may be that I
have pre-eminence in my half-magics, and that
idle persons may recall my name affably and
some one or two of the not very important
things which I did in the days of my loneliness ——"

She replied: "It is strange that in the new
spring, that even now, True Thomas, I should
be thinking about the bleak shining and about
the restlessness of a wintry sea and about a fallen
king in sober broadcloth. He is walking upon
the long marge of this sea for the while that his

aging stomach needs to digest his wholesome dinner; he belches comfortably now and then toward the sea's large restlessness; and he regards, half-idly, not any firm and ponderable thing, but only the faraway sea-mists as they rise lightly in the form of castles which he ruled in once."

He said: "But we were talking about my loneliness. All my life has been a loneliness excepting only that part I shared with you. When I left you I left the half of myself in Faëry. I came thence maimed and bedrugged and over doubtful. My fate has been the fate of all who have returned out of Faëry. I have loved nor hated nothing; I have believed nothing with any assured faith; and I have laughed without any lustiness. There has been no strength and no depth in my human living. The fervors of other men, and of the pawing women too, were a trouble to me; and I went among them warily, as must do all those who have returned from Faëry. Inside me there was only a softness and a frivolousness and a doubting in the while that

I went among these resolute and loud talking people, whose frankness I could not understand, and whose blundering wits I must ward off from ever understanding me ——"

The Queen said, "What may it avail any man to drowse in a troubled sleeping when the half of his memories live more gloriously than he lives?"

But it is ill work interrupting a poet who is about the familiar task of talking about himself. Thomas Learmont replied instantly:

"No, there are not any words. My heart understands this matter, and my heart knows very well what I am trying to tell you. But it is my mind which picks out the battered-about words that I must say to you; and since my mind does not understand this matter, it gives me the wrong words. I have not been unhappy in my human living, and I have done well enough with it, by all the measurings which are known to me. But there was something not ever found. All that has mattered in my life is that I once had your love."

So did he at last make an end of his groping speech in the while that she listened with a fond and secret smiling. Then the Queen said:

"Let us turn homeward, speaking no vain words and thinking upon no ponderable thing. Let us follow after shadows in our returning to the two we know of, in search of our ancient home. Restraint lives here, and a shrewd laborious talking makes faint my music. You nod at your frowsy hearth while the two we know of pass furtively toward the fern road that fares between heaven and hell to our ancient home. Let us be leaving this place! Here the ways of wisdom are at struggle against no ponderable thing, like shadows which war in an autumn fog, or like dead leaves scuttling and bustling aflutter to rustle in dusty gutters. So does the sound of their scuffling muffle my music. Let us be leaving this place, for its ways are dreary, and yonder lies the road to our ancient home."

Then Thomas Learmont made wide eyes at this romantic-minded and eternally young female, who was offering (in her roundabout florid fashion) to restore his own youth and the lost happiness which they had shared in Faëry. That the girl's intentions were kindly, he knew; but he knew also that she, who was immortal, could as a consequence not understand the most simple and common-sense facts.

"I am astonished," he said, and he cleared his throat,—"I am grieved, madame, that you should be suggesting any such evasion to a married man of my known principles. I most certainly could not leave the esteemed wife and the three growing sons and the other matters to which I am accustomed. I do not desire to exchange these things for more glorious things. I like to grieve over my undeservedly sad lot in life now and then, madame, because I have a poetic turn of mind: but not even in my self-pity is there much profoundness nowadays," said Thomas Learmont, with very honest regret that his lips could not lie to this eternally young person.

The Queen answered, without any smiling, as a child speaks when a puzzling world has

246

proved inexplicably unkind :"I have met in this place a corpse that is moving cumbrously; and it is hunting down a boy that thrived in the gear of all Faëry's king. Now those light sea-mists which arose like castle turrets are descending in the shape of long grave-mounds seen beyond the rim of a wintry sea; and I who am immortal turn homeward toward my own fellowship, speaking no vain words and thinking upon no ponderable thing."

Then two that had the appearance of a white hind and of a white hart came tripping down the fern road, and no sign remained anywhere of the Queen of Faëry.

Gray Thomas Learmont sighed. She was a quite charming girl, and she had meant well, and his heart was suitably ravaged with renewed anguish now that upon yet a second occasion she had passed out of his ruined living forever.

The trouble was (he reflected) that these rather flighty divine beings did not comprehend the best-thought-of human standards; and they had too a remarkably roundabout and archaic way of talking. It fitted in well enough with moonlight; still, you could not always talk in this figurative style with any imaginable woman whatever, day in and day out, and even over your porridge at breakfast, with any real comfort.

40

Is of Faded Music

IT is known that after this night Thomas Learmont went on with the course of his living. Day
in and day out he adhered to the levelness of
his life and to the practice of his half-magics,
and he took soberly the quite acceptable rewards which these magics earned toward the
discharge of his increasing household expenses,
now that two of the boys were at school. He
prospered, in so far as reached any measurings
which were ever revealed to him, in a world
wherein mortal beings rule and order matters,
and wherein he lived as neither the foremost
nor the least of his neighbors. He therefore did
not complain, since a responsible householder
could perceive nothing to complain about in
the logical daytime.

But it is known also that the infirm poet went

by moonlight to a place where three roads met
and that he made there a lament for his severance from the Queen of Faëry.

Said Thomas Learmont: "I shall not see you
any more, passing among the youthful people of
your kingdom,—that unforgotten twilit kingdom wherein all were youthful and were more
merry-hearted than are the wrangling burghers
and the broad-shouldered earls, or than are the
shining kings that prance past me upon shining
war-horses, here in earth's sunlight. It is a very
troubling sunlight. My life is a fire that dies in
this sunlight. The moments smoulder, and their
warmth dwindles in gray spirals, O Queen, in
whose fine realm there is not any gray thing nor
any sunlight."

Then Thomas Learmont said: "I shall not see
you any more, passing among the youthful people of your kingdom. In the village street I regard the comely and dear women, but not you,
—not you who were once more dear to me than
my lean heart remembers, not you whom I
found more comely than a gray brain may quite

250

believe. It is a thin sorrow to me that I do not sorrow any longer when the thought of you returns like a faded music, and awakens in me no anguish, O Queen of our young twilit realm, —for it is not anguish, a little pensively to be hearing that music's lament over my tinselled downfall into some local eminence and the respectful esteem of my fellow creatures."

And Thomas Learmont said also: "Once every dream was a sword. My dreams are not bright and keen any longer. They waver in thin spirals; and that thin thought of you, which is like an old thin music, wavers half unregarded through the ordered ways of my living. Yet at dawn it conquers me, O Queen, in the sharp gray panic of dawn. Then an aging woman sleeps on, very sturdily, at my lean side, but I may not sleep because of those little memories which nibble too closely to my lean heart. Then the dawn-wind whispers, over and over again, to the lilt of this faded music, that I shall not see you any more, passing among the youthful people of your kingdom."

251

He spoke thus with deep emotion, but he despatched no more magics in this place, since the first small magic he tried there had been successful a thought beyond his wishes. It had left him with a fret-waking suspicion that perhaps even now the unobstructed fern road before him led back to Faëry and to all which he desired.

He did not attempt to follow that road. He made his lament instead: and the dignified yet so delightfully simple phrasing of it drew tears from his old eyes, and it warmed his childish nature with a fine welling of self-pity, so that the pathos of his circumstances proved a large comfort to the infirm poet whenever his rheumatism permitted him such jaunts in the night air.

These matters are known. Yet the upshot of these matters is not known quite so certainly. Romantics declare that a hind and a hart came out of Faëry to bid Thomas Learmont cease from his play at being a well-thought-of citizen. But the conservative report that in due time he entered into eternal rest, under the proper medical attention, and that a funeral from his late residence at Ercildoune, near the Brook of Goblins, then wound up his earthly affairs without any further nonsense or any unbecoming scandal.

EXPLICIT